I0654357

Adventures

of a

Space Bum

Book 3

Finding Galium

by

Jon Batson

Midnight Whistler Publishers – since 1979

First Edition

ISBN-13: 978-0989372633
ISBN-10: 0989372634

Midnight Whistler Publishers
http://www.midnightwhistler.com
info@midnightwhistler.com

Cover Art by

BREAKIRON ®
Animation&Design
www.breakiron.com

Adventures of a Space Bum

book 3

Finding Galium

Glossary

Abigail — Starwort's friend from school, named Father's joy

Anubis — In Egyptian mythology, god of the dead. It is the name of a planet in the middle ring.

Aristaeus — Doctor Genus, named for the Greek god, son of Apollo

Bacchus — Starwort's family name, in Greek and Roman mythology, god of wine. Also, home planet named for the family Bacchus.

Be-demoned! — Exclamation of having erred in judgment

Borth — A large and angry dog used to guard locations. (Borth stool: what this animal leaves behind him.)

Cecrops — A planet with two cities: Daedalus and Icarus

Chineel — First mate, Starwort's aunt, named for the Manchineel flower.

CG — Central Government of Earth, an oppressive body.

Chandler — Purveyor of ship's goods and supplies

Copernicus — A planetary town named for Copernicus, the founder of modern astronomy

Crinole — A flower signifying *delicate weakness*

Daedalus — A city named for a respected Athenian artisan

Dagon — Name of a crewman, for the Philistine fish-god

Daphne	School friend of Starwort's, still living on Khons, the home planet.
Dash-wire	A portable portal for carrying data
Datur	Thornapple plant, signifying *deceitful charms*
Daughter of Ra!	Exclamation bordering on profanity
Flax	Name of the entity of the vessel, after a flower meaning benefactor "I will call you Flax, for you are my benefactor."
Galium	Friend from Sterope, named for a flower signifying rudeness
Gold-backs	Slang for Universals
Grecian Flu	An illness created by the Central Government to control the population
Hephae	A mercenary named for Hephaestus, Greek god of fire
Hermes	In Greek mythology, messenger of the gods, in this story, a GPS unit, a tracking device.
Indran Storm	A storm named for Indra, the Vedic god of storms, rain and battle.
Inner Ring	Planets close to Earth and under control of the Central Government.
Juno	Largest city on the planet Jove.
Khons	A planet named for the Egyptian god of the chase.
Kronos	An exclamation, ex: "for Kronos sake!"
Kronos Chiropteran	A bat native to the planet Kronos
Levitator	An elevator
Malameris	Shapeless aquatics, a delicacy with a deadly sting
Manchineel	The name of Starwort's aunt, a flower meaning "betrayal"

Mithra Tavern A tavern on Sterope, named after the goddess of mediation

New Babylon A planet with both low-life bars and healing pools.

Ortie French for the nettle flower, signifying *cruelty.*

Osiris V Brand and designation for a speeder, popular at the time

Pallas A planet named for Pallas Athena, Greek godess of war.

Phorcys and Ceto! Exclamation bordering on profanity

RRD Remote Repair Drone

Seb President of the Central Government on Earth

Semper Adonis A name used by Galium, from Semper, Latin for forever, and Adonis, the name of the beautiful Roman god.

Souci French for Marigold, a flower that could mean foresight, but could also mean trouble

Starwort Name of a low-growing north temperate herb having small white star-shaped flowers. Meaning: afterthought.

Sterope An island on New Babylon, named after one of the Pleiades

Trebium Scuttle A part no longer used on vessels

Universals Denomination of money common to all worlds, using the symbol Ⱶ as in Ⱶ20

Victoriana The planet where Dr. Genus lives.

Wind Pools Expensive resort at New Babylon, famous for its healing vapors.

Adventures

of a

Space Bum

Book 3

Finding Galium

Starwort (stärwôrt) n. Any of various water plants having star-shaped flowers. Also, low-growing north temperate herb having small white star-shaped flowers; named for its ability to ease sharp pains in the side. Significance: Afterthought

"I got a tattoo: a tiny, white, star-shaped flower on my left shoulder blade. It was to remind me that I am a weed growing in still waters. So I kept moving, avoiding the still waters; vowing to be a weed no more."

Starwort Bacchus

Still Flying

"Klack!"

My stick came down hard aiming for Dagon's head. His own stick rose to meet mine, stopping it in the air an inch before the target. Dagon was quick and swung his weapon wide around his head. I guessed at the trajectory and put mine in the way before my face was smashed by the blow.

"Klack!"

Dagon watched my eyes. Was I giving my next move away? I swung my stick directly at the side of his head, the shortest route, but he was still ahead of me. A short, tight circle around his head brought his stick directly in the path of my own.

"Throng!" My stick shattered on Dagon's, rendering it useless. The stroke took the boy soldier by surprise. He had been a fighter since he could crawl on a planet always at war. He was not used to losing, he was used to standing victorious over a fallen foe.

"That's enough, you two. You're scaring me."

The voice from the galley was that of Chineel. Red haired and handsome, she was my first mate and handy in the galley, which was good because I was not. She was also a woman of the world; scaring her was not an easy task.

The fourth member of our crew is Flax, the ship's computer. Though to say Flax is the ship's computer is rather like saying the universe is big. Flax had long since outrun every advanced computer system there was. She made her own decisions and had her own opinions. Today, her opinion was heard loud and clear.

"I was enjoying the contest. I believe Starwort is getting better at this. She almost had you, Dagon."

"Well, my money is on Dagon every time," said Chineel.

"Still," said Dagon, pausing to catch his breath. "It's time for a break, or lunch, whatever will qualify. You had me on the run, Captain."

"High praise indeed, from the most formidable soldier I know. Yes, time for a break."

Flax's holographic head, that of a comely woman about Chineel's age, disappeared from the galley console. I knew it was visible on the bridge, watching the stars as they came toward us. Of course, she didn't watch them. She was a holograph to make interface with the crew easier. And the stars didn't come toward us, we flew at them, though some were ancient suns burnt out millions of years earlier, their light just reaching us.

"Tell me why we're going again?" queried Dagon as he settled in at the main galley table.

"Galium's message is cryptic, but the coordinates are not, they point to Cecrops. We're going to find him. Once I see he is all right, we can go where we please."

"The usual precautions?"

"No, I don't think so. Daedalus is not a Central Government outpost and the sister city of Icarus is a resort town. The most danger we will find is overspending and overeating."

After lunch, I retired to the bridge, to my thinking zone and remembered Galium: curt, wonderful Galium. The man I called the rude pirate of Sterope was one of the first friends I made after my escape from the girls academy on Khons. He accepted me immediately into his circle of friends and insisted everyone do the same. The only drawback was that he loved calling me "Little Wort."

Captain Starwort Bacchus

The low islands of my youth, called the Daughters, were far away on New Babylon. The Winged Maidens: Sterope, Terpsichore, Melpomene, and all the rest, were left, along with Galium, behind me. It had been nearly three winters since I left school – late at night and out of options.

The bridge was my thinking place. Surrounded by the light of a million stars, I could free my mind enough to see the past and the present clearly, maybe even enough to gain a glimpse of the future.

"Where are we going, Captain?" Chineel asked, settling into the co-pilot's seat.

"Cecrops, a planet named for the mythical first king of Athens. The coordinates hidden in Galium's cryptic message takes us there."

"That's all we know?"

"That's all we know."

A holographic face appeared on the console as if waking from slumber. The newly acquired face of Flax blinked soft hazel eyes and smiled to set her crew at ease.

"We know a great deal more, Captain. Though the coordinates were all I could learn from his message, Galium has been sending bits of encrypted information out to the universe for several months, all intended for you, it seems."

"For me?" It was the first I knew. I had spoken with him on the interlink and he had given me some valuable information more than once. The old pirate I knew from Sterope had mellowed with age, though he still called me by the name he so loved, the one I hated.

"The messages were targeted for Little Wort. Is that not the name he called you several times?"

"Yes, he called me that, though I asked him not to."

"As I understand it, Galium has little regard for what others ask of him."

"Yes. He is his own man, that's for sure. Replay his first message, would you, Flax?"

Flax flashed Galium's familiar visage on the main screen, larger than life, like the man. The message played, but it was not a video transmission, it was a voice recording.

"Hello. So glad you could call. Things are a little hectic at these coordinates, so if you could call later, I'd appreciate it." His voice sounded strained, not easy as he usually was. Galium was a man always in control of his situation. Apparently that had changed.

"Now the second message, please?" I asked Flax.

"...these coordinates, so if you could call... Click! ...these coordinates, so if you could call... Click! ...these coordinates, so if you could call..."

"Thank you, Flax."

"There are coordinates for Cecrops embedded in the message. That is our destination," Flax said.

"What do the other messages say?"

"A location for a city called Icarus,"

"In Earth mythology, the son of Daedalus."

"Yes. There is also a city named Daedalus on the planet."

I turned, looking into the holographic eyes of my friend, the artificial intelligence setting the new standard out on the ragged edge of the known universe.

"Is Daedalus on our itinerary?"

"No, Captain, we have no plans to go to Daedalus."

"What else does he say in his messages?"

"Warnings about the Grecian Flu, to travel wide of the Central Government, which has your name on a list of wanted individuals, though it seems the picture is that of someone else."

I smiled. Flax saw my smile and queried.

"Captain?" Flax said.

"Galium couldn't remove the file, but he could alter the associated picture. He changed yours as well."

Lights blinked as Flax pulled up a list of wanted individuals from recent ports we had visited. There were many names listed, more with each new release, until my own name was buried in the avalanche of names and pictures. On the main screen, a likeness appeared of a gun ship twice the size of Flax and bristling with munitions large and small. "Gun Ship used by fugitive Bacchus" it said on the bottom of the picture.

"Can you do something about that?" I asked.

"Affirmative. The file is old, but is still a part of the record. It is more difficult to remove an old file than a recent one. Let me see what I can do."

"How long will it take?"

7

"It was done when you asked."

"Now you're just showing off," I said, smiling at my friend's image.

"There was also a message concerning the planet Bacchus. If I had uncovered it sooner, our visit would have had a different context."

Again, Galium's face appeared on the main screen, only this time tired and worn. He was growing weary of the chase.

"Hello, Little Wort. On your way to Bacchus? Your father's gift of an entire planet will be a disappointment, I fear. There's nothing there at the landing platform, Wort. It's an empty desert, a desolate wasteland as far as the eye can see. But that is the trick, isn't it? How far can the eye see? Consider that when looking. There might be more to it on the other side of the frame line. Oop! I have to take my leave. Fly knowingly, Wort!"

The screen went blank. I took a deep breath.

"Is that dated, Flax?"

"At the time of our takeoff from Victoriana, Captain."

"How long until we reach Cecrops, Flax?"

"Seven days nav-time."

"I have to think about this."

"Yes, Captain."

Flax turned her head to look out at the universe as we flew toward coordinates given us in a cryptic message by an old friend, a rude pirate from my early days.

Family

From the pilot seat on the bridge, the universe was visible in all its glory. The Red Stroke Drive propelled us through the blackness at a speed unheard of in my early childhood. Galaxies of many colors came into view and disappeared again. Like the milestones of my life they appeared, showed their colors and were left behind, living only in memory.

I looked to my right, at Chineel sitting in the co-pilot seat. She didn't have the smallest idea what the dots and lights surrounding her did. If she had to co-pilot the vessel anywhere, she would be at a loss.

Chineel came aboard a winter ago and took over the galley and stores, a good friend and companion. In a fight, she's invaluable. Like myself, Chineel had come a long way from the Mithra Tavern where I found her. Before that she was married to my uncle, the one who gave me the scar just above my left collar bone, the one I cover in most ports. Only in places where your scar is a sign of your liberation, your freedom from the implanted chip of the Central Government, did I let my scar show.

Chineel had guessed from our conversations that her husband, my uncle, was dead. She never asked how he died or who was responsible for his eventual demise. I was glad she didn't ask and gladder still she didn't guess.

The memory of my uncle on the floor of the great room, the neck of a whiskey bottle twisted into his eye and the iron rod from the fire driven into his head, came back to me. I sucked in a bellyful of air and pushed the memory out. I was not yet out of school at the time, still a young child.

As if a change of scenery would change my memory, I stood and walked back to the galley. Chineel came with me, as she was not needed on the bridge but might be needed in the galley. She walked at my side through the port bay. Her long skirt, predictably green to accent her red hair, swished with each step.

Chineel was loyal no matter what and had faced death and worse in my company. Her name, short for Manchineel, a flower signifying betrayal, had no bearing on her life at all. As she would say, what's in a name?

Dagon sat at the galley table reading from one of the workable slats from the library. He looked up as his Captain walked in. He closed the slat and prepared to stand, ready to serve if there were orders.

"No, Dagon, don't get up. I'm just here to think and to have a cup of something warm and stimulating."

Dagon sat back down, returning to his slat, while Chineel turned to the counter to locate the object of my request. I sat at the far end of the table, watching Dagon read, watching Chineel as she bustled around the cupboards and canisters preparing my drink.

This was my family. All the family I had left. All the family I would need.

There were others who qualified, of course. There was Aristaeus, a technical genius and good friend who lived on Victoriana. We had an open invitation to visit, or to live there forever if we liked.

Galium was family, if I was honest with myself. He wouldn't agree, because that would be the amiable thing to do. Galium was never amiable, that was Jessamine.

Jessamine and her constant companion, Papa Posei, were the first to welcome me into the low islands. Jessamine insisted I wash my hands before I ate. She and Papa Posei were like second parents to me.

And Galium was family, not for any other reason than he always looked out for me, even after I left him. There were many times I wished I had him back, only to realize that it was not Galium I missed, but the idea of him. I missed having someone kind, who cared, who loved me and wished only the best for me, but someone who wouldn't call me "Wort."

"What do you want, Star?" Chineel asked.

I looked up at Chineel, though I was unable to speak through trembling lips. I must have looked like a lost puppy, because she came over to me and wrapped her arms around me.

"Oh, sweetness, no, don't do that, don't sink into those feelings. I only meant, what can I get you? Come on, shake it off, take a breath." Chineel took my face in two hands. "Breathe, Star, breathe!"

I laughed through my tears and threw my arms around her, pressed against her bosom. Through my one open eye, I saw Dagon looking at us, not knowing what to do.

Dagon, the boy soldier we rescued from Pallas, the planet no longer at war, had no experience to deal with feelings such as these. He needed someone to explain what was happening, or perhaps subtitles. He wanted to help his Captain and his First Mate, but didn't know how. He was unequipped for emotions.

Ubiquitous Flax smiled at us from the console, tested the air and raised the temperature a degree.

This was my family, the only family I had and the only family I would ever need.

Cecrops

In the primary city of Daedalus on the planet Cecrops, where the Central Government had not yet planted a steel boot, stood a town center of immense proportions. The tower at the focal point stood eight hundred meters into the sky topped by a mushroom-shaped dome bristling with antennae and circled by windows featuring breathtaking views of the city below. The main city, the inner ring, was the business center, with structures reaching up to dizzying heights. Between these buildings ran a network of streets bustling with traffic from dawn to dusk.

In the darkness, the streets were empty and black, and night held dominion, no one ventured into the inner ring. The three outer rings were where the people lived, in rows of houses, large and small.

Those who stayed home in the outer rings never ventured into the inner city, into the downtown central circle. This was a city where people kept to themselves.

The outlying spires of Daedalus gathered information from the planets and relayed it to the antennas atop the giant dome. In the many windows, workers labored over the information without ever looking out at the scenic view they shared. The ever-present clouds covering the three outer circles obscured the view, so it didn't matter if they looked, much of the time they saw only clouds.

The outlying spires also had offices, much like grand headquarters of fine companies and organizations such as occupied the central dome. Many of these offices were let to independent businessmen and smaller companies. In one of these, Datur Minot, named Datur by his family for the thornapple plant, signifying *deceitful charms*, made his headquarters. No doubt his family was unaware of the name's meaning at the time.

Datur Minot had been for some time working on a project, a project that was proving to take longer than intended. He was becoming impatient with the lack of results.

"This time I can almost taste it!" he told his bot assistant, K4D Tertiary. "We've come close before, but that was with lesser men. She won't escape me this time."

Tertiary stood four feet tall and was metal from his oval head to his three nobbled toes on each foot. His arms swung from his shoulders to his knees, giving the impression of being a robotic ape. Tertiary had no voice box, no vocal ability, and so said nothing in reply.

"Damn that girl!" cried out Datur Minot. "And all who sail with her."

Tertiary rotated on his pelvis to turn his single viewing orb to his master. Datur's expression gave him no clue as to what he was damning these people for.

Datur was not much taller than his robot, standing an inch short of five feet. His slender frame seemed to bend under the weight of his cotton shirt and pants, pulled in at the waist to fit his narrow middle. His white hair grew raggedly from ear to ear around the back of his head. Several eye operations did not spare him from having to wear heavy spectacles when he worked. All these things considered, Datur Minot did not look like a criminal mastermind, and yet considered himself to be exactly that. All he needed now was a henchmen he could trust. Those were hard to find.

The silence of his office was broken by the sudden ringing of an alarm. Datur reached over and brushed the dot on Tertiary's side to silence the alarm. He looked at the readout on his holoscreen, floating an inch above his work-desk. A mercenary recruit known only as Hephae, after Hephaestus, the Greek god of fire, was ascending in the levitator.

"Open the doors," Datur said to Tertiary. Tertiary swiveled his head in the direction of the levitator doors and activated an internal switch.

As the levitator came to a halt on the top story of the spire, the doors opened. A man nearly twice the size of Datur stepped out and walked to the center of the office. He wore a gray standard two-piece business suit over a muscular body. His face was calm, his eyes disinterested.

"Take a seat," said Datur, indicating a chair. He hoped it would hold the big man. Datur noted that the suit was cut wide at the chest to accommodate a blaster carried in a shoulder holster.

"I'm not cheap," said Hephae, as the chair creaked beneath his weight.

"I'm not looking for cheap, I'm looking for effective. Can you get a job done?"

The big man spoke quietly, softly. He didn't need to raise his voice to be heard or be forceful to be taken seriously.

"I can do the job you need. Of course, I would need to know what the job is."

"Someone I have located has information I need. You will go and get it. There may be some coercion involved. I trust you're up to that?"

"Coercion is not a problem. Neither is disposal of the witnesses afterwards, if you require."

"Yes. There may be some witness removal needed. There are others who travel with her."

"Her?" Hephae narrowed his eyes. "A woman?"

"A woman, more like a girl, but she has some powerful friends. The treasure in question is the inheritance left to her by her father. There is a great deal of money but there is also land, including a rather large planet."

"He left her a planet?"

"Yes, a whole planet."

"So, I have to go to this planet?"

"No, she isn't there."

"So you want me to find her and kill her?"

"No, not kill her. Not yet, that is. First we need the information she has. I can find her, I can tell you where she will be and who will be with her. You can take her and get the data from her concerning her money and holdings. This girl has proven most resourceful. There must be a way to access her accounts and find her deeds."

"There are deeds? Property? I heard that property has become a thing of the past, that no one owns land anymore."

"Central Government brainwashing. They want you to think you can't own anything so it doesn't matter if they take it away from you. Trust me, deeds are still valuable."

"You said a girl. You said it once before."

"Yes, a girl, for Kronos' sake! But with lots of help and she's smart. You can't go up against someone like her and expect to win just because you're strong or have a gun. You have to be able to think."

"You don't deal with confrontation well, do you?" Hephae goaded.

"Don't make the mistake of underestimating her, or me for that matter. There is more at work here than mere brains or brawn, there is something super-natural about her."

"What makes you believe you can ensnare her when others have not?"

"For one thing, I now have you. You're smarter and stronger than any who have gone against her before." Datur flattered the brawny fellow hoping he would take the job and not leave him without options.

"And another thing?" asked Hephae, accepting his superior strength and intelligence as given, but anticipating another shoe to drop.

"She's coming here."

"Here?" Hephae pointed to the spot between his boots.

"Here to Cecrops, to Icarus. I sent her a message ensuring her arrival. She is on the way now, flying into our nets. We don't have to chase her all over the universe, she is coming to us. The trap is set."

Icarus

The city named for the boy who flew too close to the sun was the smaller of the two cities on Cecrops. The larger, Daedalus, was a major space port able to handle the comings and goings of the surrounding five galaxies with ease. Icarus, on the other hand, was for tourists, those seeking a small, quaint, as yet untouched place to visit on a honeymoon or romantic vacation. Icarus was a place for lovers.

As Flax descended onto the skyport at Icarus, she gave us a glimpse of an island city covered in mist. The low cloud formations were due partly to the high elevation of the city itself and partly due to the weather of Cecrops. Rain was a regular occurrence, though usually over and done within minutes. It was also predictable, as storms invariably began in Daedalus and swept west to Icarus.

Below the cloud cover, a bustling city came alive before us. A twenty-story hotel attached to the port boasted a dozen minarets and a bridge over a waterway allowing even tall ships to enter the bay.

The bay itself was designed for swimming as well as the docking of boats, big and small. Several one-and-two-person sailboats cruised the bay at leisure while bathers of every description lounged on the sandy beach across the road from the hotel.

The lower floors of the hotel were for events, going up seven stories before the guest floors began. In the skies overhead, slow-moving airships cruised from their docking pins to broader platforms allowing guests to visit the many splendors of Icarus.

"There is where you will find him," Flax said, with a nod to the large hotel. One of those seven hundred rooms was Galium's secret headquarters, according to her location system.

"Shall we knock?" I asked, looking for an approach that wouldn't give away our intent.

"He knows you're coming. The decoy animal has been freed from the container. Is that correct?"

asked Flax. She worked on her conversational abilities at every opportunity.

"You mean, 'the cat is out of the bag?' Yes, that's mostly right."

"Then I don't understand," said Flax, a perplexed look on the holographic face. "Why should a cat be in the bag in the first place?"

"It's an old marketplace reference. If one wanted to buy a small pig, one could buy, as they said then, 'a pig in a poke' or bag. If the seller could switch bags, you would arrive home to let the cat out and the subterfuge would be revealed."

"I see," Flax said, her face taking on the expression of understanding the reference. "So, if you have paid for a small pig in a bag without knowing you brought home a cat, which would still move about in the bag, you would be cheated. I assume, therefore, the cat is less valuable than the pig."

"Yes. You wouldn't eat a cat."

"I would not, but there are those who do. Some cultures will cook a common house cat and eat it with items from the garden. Many Eastern cultures of early Earth are said to have eaten animals used in the west as domesticated pets."

"Let's be clear: We're not eating cats aboard this vessel, not while I'm Captain."

"Who's eating cats?" Chineel asked, entering the bridge and the conversation simultaneously.

"No one," I replied. "And it's going to stay that way. We're changing the subject now. How do we get to the hotel from the skyport?"

"It's close enough that one could walk if the weather is fair."

"Will I need an identity chip?" In places where a chip is needed, the Central Government Terminal Secure Agents stood by the line hoping to make an arrest and claim the bonus a good arrest brought with it.

"You will have an identity chip for Souci Bach. In this port, it would not be good to use your name. Though on the edge of the middle ring, they do get alerts from time to time."

Flax had fashioned a chip for the name I had used before in several ports where my own might raise an eyebrow. If anyone was looking closely, Souci Bach would not attract interest. Starwort Bacchus would do so without much searching.

"And you're sure this is the location where we'll find the old pirate, Galium?"

"These are the coordinates," Flax nodded.

"Not Daedalus? It seems to me Daedalus would be more his style."

"No. Daedalus is the capital and certainly would be more like him, from what you have told me. When I opened his encryption, Icarus was the name of the town, not Daedalus."

"Dagon," I called to my personal bodyguard. "Dress for a holiday; today you are a tourist."

"What does a tourist wear?"

"It's a tourist port, so anything goes."

The King Minos Hotel

"We could land Flax in here," I said as we walked into the vast lobby of the King Minos Hotel. The ceiling was so high, I couldn't make out the details of the art depicted there. It looked like a series of beautiful women in various unnatural poses, all nude, covered only partly by scarves and drapes. Dagon took particular notice.

"Where are Galium's quarters?" Chineel asked.

"Top floor, in the back, according to this readout."

Flax had equipped me with a Hermes complete with the location of the coordinates, down to the rooms in the hotel.

"We should have no trouble finding him. This way, Dagon. Dagon?" I had to press the point.

"Yes! Of course! This way." Dagon followed me, still glancing back and up at the half-dressed maidens on the lobby ceiling.

Chineel looked at me with a roll of her eyes. Her whole demeanor seemed to say, "Boys!" Of course, Dagon was still a boy in the physical sense, but had been a soldier since his first step. He was not one to be trifled with. I had to remind myself that he was fast becoming a man.

The levitator soared upwards with greater speed than I would have liked, depositing us on the upper resident floor of the hotel. The winding corridors seemed to go on forever, twisting and turning, bringing us to a junction where we expected another hall but found instead a window to the world.

Out of the window, far below and between the clouds, the city of Icarus spread out, winding streets echoing the layout of the hotel hallways, houses next to office buildings, habitats with shops and bistros squeezed in between them. There seemed to be no logical explanation to the town below us.

Every street was clogged with ground vehicles. Many of the hovercraft and speeders were similar in color, brightly painted to attract attention.

"They must be for hire," Chineel said, pointing.

"Yes, and some are larger, delivery vans I suppose. The remaining seem to be private vehicles, but they are all confined to the ground."

We turned our gaze to the air. In the distance at our same height and even higher, air-ships floated slowly along, held aloft by large balloons tied with ropes. Their gondolas were as large as a troop carrier or larger, festooned with ribbons and draped with banners.

"The skies are reserved for tourist traffic, sightseeing and the like," I ventured.

"We must take a trip on one of those," Chineel said. "How exciting!"

"Oh? Because we find life to be so boring and hum-drum on an interplanetary craft, that flying in a slow-moving airship would be an interesting change?" I looked at her with amazement.

"No need for sarcasm. It looks fun, is all. Let's find Galium."

"Good idea." I turned back up the corridor with the Hermes in my hand, following the red blip to the door we sought.

The blip sped up, as if excited as we got close to our goal. Around another corner and... nothing! We stood at a blank wall.

"This can't be it," Chineel said.

"The Hermes says it is."

"Then the Hermes is wrong."

We stood before the blank wall, it's clean lines broken only by a predictable picture of a seascape and a short table bearing a pot of red and gold flowers.

Dagon began feeling the sides of the walls and beneath the table. He felt behind the frame of the picture, which was secure to the wall. He pulled at the frame and pushed the molding at the edge of the wall.

We all jumped when a groaning sound came from the wall and it moved back, opening as if on wheels, hinged at one side. It continued its slow swing until there was room for the three of us to walk inside one at a time, and then stopped. No further sound came from within the dark space.

Dagon produced a pocket light and took the lead. Chineel followed him and I brought up the rear, looking behind me as I entered. There was no one in the hall behind us, no one to see where we had gone. I wondered if that was good or bad. If the wall closed us in, no one would know we were inside. On the other hand, if this was indeed where Galium worked, it was better that no one else knew about it.

Once in, Dagon found a switch, illuminating a wide hallway, carpeted in dark gray fabric and leading to a brighter glow at the end.

Dagon pushed on as I turned to close the wall behind us, sealing us in and the world out.

The glow was the light of a decorated living room, with windows to the outside and like any other in the hotel. Stuffed chairs and a large sofa formed the center of the room with quaint tables to hand at each. On the wall opposite the sofa was a viewing screen, dark, and a control disk on the side table by the nearest chair.

Chineel ran a finger along one of the tables and held it up for me to see. Dust clung to the pad of her finger. "No one's cleaned in a while. Perhaps this one doesn't get maid service."

Dagon noted two doorways, neither of which had a door to close, one leading to a sleep chamber and the other to a stylized galley area, a food preparation room.

"A kitchen, I believe is the colloquial term," Chineel said, sizing up the counter space and central prep table.

"Let's see what's there," I said, pointing to the closed door on the other side of the food prep room.

Dagon took the lead again, walking across the kitchen, but stopped, as if he had frozen in space. He raised a hand, indicating we should also stop. He stood with one foot still raised, as if his next step could not happen. He looked down, then back at me. He pointed to the floor.

There across the floor at a height of two inches, was a thin glow, a nearly imperceptible change of the light from the prep table to the cupboard against the wall.

Trip-beam

Dagon motioned us back with a slow wave of his fingers. Chineel backed up into the main room. I followed her, walking backwards and looking over my shoulder for other indications of either alarms or traps.

Dagon bent down and opened the cupboard. Inside he saw a series of power relays coupled with a detonator. He stood and stepped back from the slender glow, thinner than a spider's thread.

"How did you see that?" I asked.

"I used to set them up back on Pallas."

"Knowledge comes in handy, sometimes."

"Captain, I suggest we remove ourselves," Dagon said in a whisper. I nodded.

No further word was needed. Dagon turned Chineel around and guided her to the moving wall as I brought up the rear. We exited the wall and returned it to its position, appearing as if nothing at all was there except a wall.

The journey to the lobby was quicker now, as we knew the way without side trips and dead ends. Through the lobby, Dagon didn't even glance up to see the half-clad ladies draped across the ceiling. Our goal was the entrance and nothing would slow our progress.

At the elaborate front doors, we stood looking in different directions, taking the entire landscape in, looking for who might be looking for us. Chineel surveyed the swimming area off to the right, consisting of bathers, some seeking the open light and others under canopies. Two venders hawked their wares, one selling drink and the other wrapped delicacies large and small. In the distance, several more carts and kiosks catered to the crowds of tourists.

I scanned the bay before the entrance, the small boats under sail and smaller ones paddled. No one seemed to take interest in us.

Dagon looked left to the port entrance and the hotel as it wrapped around the near shore, bridged the entrance and continued on the far shore. He could see nothing of interest in the hotel or the port entrance.

High above, an airship lifted off, its gondola filled with tourists and vacationers eager for a sky-view of Icarus. Nothing seemed out of place, nothing was amiss.

"Anything?" I asked Dagon.

"No, Captain."

"Or here," Chineel added.

"Galium would not have directed us to this place and then set a trip-beam. Or if he had, he would have warned us. This is a diversion."

"I agree, Captain," Dagon said.

"Chineel, will you go back to Flax? Monitor communications and send us any information you find. You're our eyes and ears at the skyport. Dagon, you will go along the shore to the left. Look for any sign. Report what you find. I'll go to the right and into town. Galium isn't just clever, he's downright sneaky. If there's a way to get us a message, he'll utilize it."

Without further word, we left in our diverse directions, Chineel walking with Dagon to the far side of the hotel, where the road to the skyport split off. I walked to the right, past the vendors selling drinks and treats, past the canopies and bathers in chairs, along the avenue called Portside Walk according to the sign, and into the town of Icarus.

Head First

High in the spire on the edge of Daedalus, an alarm went off loud enough to hear in any part of the office, but particularly loud to those standing next to the robot, Tertiary.

"Let's just dive in, head first, as it were," Datur Minot said to the soldier of fortune, Hephae. "If you can guarantee you'll get the job done, I know where the girl is now and where she probably is going. I have a lock on her pocket communicator." Datur unrolled a folio, a large reader of stiff plasticast. He pressed the start dot and the folio lit up.

"What's this?" asked Hephae.

"Map of Icarus. Here is the landing platform and skyport. By tracking communications to and from their vessel as well as their pocket communicator, we'll know where they are at all times. They have just been here: the hotel. They clearly didn't find what they want, nor did they trip the stun-trap."

"So now what?"

"They'll continue to look for their friend and we will track them in town. If they leave we can track them in the sky."

"And once we find them?"

"The girl is the key. There is a woman with her, but she is of no consequence. There is a boy as well, but he is, after all, only a child. They are not our concern. The girl knows where the money is and where the deeds are. What other treasures comprise her inheritance, I don't know, but she does have some money. She bought her Exterra vessel at twice what it was worth. You don't throw that kind of money around unless you have mountains of it."

"Who is she?" The big man placed a hand on the table and leaned his weight against it, making Datur concerned for the table, which wasn't made for such a load.

"Let's go over here and sit down. Would you like some morning ale?"

Datur walked Hephae to the corner conversation area, with comfortable chairs and a low table. Tertiary went to the preparation chamber for drinks.

"She is the only daughter of two notable doctors, renowned in their fields and highly successful. The estate they left her is, I was told, a fortune one could not spend in ten lifetimes. She traveled for a while and never worked long at anything. She didn't have to. I suppose she took jobs just for the fun of it."

"And now she has her own vessel?"

"Yes, which she rules with an iron fist as Captain. She has become a pirate, which means she probably has ill-gotten riches on board as well. She might like the adventure of it all, but make no mistake, there is money there. She keeps the woman and the boy as servants. They have to be expensive."

"So, just a girl. Your former associates couldn't take down this girl? Is there some form of martial arts at play? Is she a trained fighter?"

"There is no history of it."

"Weapons expert?"

"Again, nothing in the records, nor is there a trail of bullet-riddled bodies."

"You said a couple of henchmen were killed," Hephae darkened.

"Well, one or two perhaps, but nothing to suggest a pattern."

"One or two? One is enough if it's you."

"She was approached by three men in a refresh room. She shot two of them with the third man's gun. One died, the other was wounded and got away."

"So he's still alive?"

"No, killed by security guards at the shopping plaza."

"And did the third man live?"

"No, he was killed by the other two. She held him in front ... It really doesn't matter about them."

Datur was tired of all the questions. He stabbed the map with a bony finger.

"Look! She's here! She's only got these two for help. There's no evidence of a weapon and she's even traveling under another name, so she will most likely not contact the authorities for help in a pinch. I've been tracking her. I'll tell you where she is, you go and get her. Your cut will make you rich beyond your dreams."

"What is my cut?" Hephae had taken work before without asking and was unhappy with the result.

"Thirty percent. I've spent a lot of time on this girl."

"I want fifty. Half, or do your own dirty work."

"Thirty-five percent and it's hardly any work at all, none of it dirty. Thirty-five percent will make you rich for the rest of your life."

"Forty-five." Hephae leaned forward, fast growing impatient. He wanted more.

"Forty. That's the extent of my generosity. Forty and get on with it, or go. Your choice."

Hephae leaned back and sighed. The low, guttural groan seemed to Datur to go on for minutes, but was in fact was a mere few seconds.

"Where do I begin?"

"She and her friends came here to meet with an old friend at the hotel by the bay. When she discovered he wasn't there, she walked from the skyport and is still walking through town. I'll give you a sonic connector and tracker. Find her and bring her here for interrogation. Disable the other two if they are with her. Once we have the accounts and access codes, the deeds and interlinks, we will have all we need and she will no longer be of use."

"We'll dispose of her?" Hephae asked.

"It's a deep bay," Datur replied. Deep enough for both of you, Datur thought.

Honor

It was mid-morning in Icarus. The early meal was a thing of memory and the mid-day meal was still two hours off. Restaurants I passed were closed, though workers inside bustled about, cleaning tables and preparing for the rush at mid-day.

Cafes were in full swing, however, bulging with tourists and people with little to do but to sit around and discuss what they didn't do yesterday.

Music caught my attention and I hurried to the next corner to see what was coming. To my surprise, it was a wedding party, bride and groom dressed in their finest followed by friends and family, a five piece walking band and children carrying garlands of flowers and ribbons of all colors.

The wedding procession continued along Portside Walk, turning just beyond the bay to pass three ornate cathedrals on the right and an airship slip on the left.

The airship was a huge, wooden boat, capable of holding a hundred people easily, buoyed up by a stitched airbag longer than the boat and held on by ropes. It inched into the slip as men with hooks and ropes stood at the sides to secure the vessel. It was a slow-motion ballet of men and airship, one so common in Icarus that no one turned to watch save for me. I alone stood gawking at the behemoth as it drifted into its port and came to a stop. A walkway was lowered and smiling passengers disembarked, chatting amiably about what they had seen from high above the city.

I continued following the wedding party along the broad avenue to the entrance of a garden decorated in paper flowers and ribbons, all of white. The ladies were all in long dresses with hoops and frills, each a different color. The men were in suits with coats and colorful shirts, flowers decorated the lapels. Every face wore a smile.

The island of people all moving at once carried me into the garden and deposited me before a table overflowing with food and drink. There were complete wheels of cheese, cut vegetables and bowls of whipped paste to dip them in. Sliced meats graced one large platter while fruit of every description filled another. A girl with a tray walked by me, stopped and offered me a treat: a piece of fish with cheese and a slice of fruit, all on a triangle cracker. It looked good, so I took one. It was a delicacy! I had not tasted the like since the low islands of New Babylon.

"You have traveled far and are comely when polished," said a voice strangely familiar. I turned and looked into the handsome face of a young man I didn't recognize. He had neatly combed hair of dark brown, was clean shaven and smiled with flawless teeth of sparkling white. He was dressed in a two-piece suit with a white shirt buttoned to the throat with a deep blue oval stone in place of the button. In his breast pocket was a red, silk handkerchief.

"Do I know you, sir?"

He bowed in ancient fashion. "You do, miss. I had the honor of your presence in a drinking establishment on Ceres Segundo. I believe I offered you a job."

It was the Sector Agent I had met in the tavern when Flax repaired the communications array on Ceres. He had been covered with the dust of a dozen planets and at least a three-day-growth of beard, yet was handsome still. I had thought of him many times since.

"You were chasing your man. I think there was a fight, wasn't there?" I was trying to remember the meeting and not the dreams I had of him offering me highly personal invitations to sweeten my slumber.

"He held you in a powerful grip, and yet you prevailed. As I recall you stomped on his foot, broke his nose with your head and put a boot between his legs. He turned the most handsome shade of purple."

The Sector Agent smiled, remembering our first meeting so well, better than I, in fact. Clearly, I had made an impression on him, as he did on me.

"Had I not had places to go, I might have taken you up on your offer to join the agents."

"Just as well you didn't, they would have sent us to different stations. I wouldn't have cared for that."

His smile was intoxicating. My head swam and I struggled to keep standing. I wanted to fall into his arms and drift off into the clouds on a romantic airship.

"Nor I," I said, far too enthusiastically. I recovered quickly. "That is, your offer seemed to be to take me under your wing, to show me the way of the Sector Agent. To be sent just anywhere and far from you, wouldn't, well..."

"Wouldn't be what we had in mind," he finished my sentence far more adroitly than I could have.

"Yes. That's what I meant."

"Honor Toth," the Sector Agent said, holding out a hand to me. I looked at the hand, wanting to fall into it and wrap it around me. Instead I took his hand in mine and shook it firmly, as if we were finalizing a business arrangement.

"Souci Bach. Please tell me this isn't your wedding. I would be horrified if I met you again on your wedding day before we got to know each other." I blushed at my bold words, but held his gaze.

"Uh, no," he stammered, caught off guard. "A friend. It's a friend of mine getting married, not me. No, not yet, at least."

"Oh? Do you have a wedding planned? Should I buy a gift for someone special?"

"No, Miss Bach, nothing planned, no one special. The life of a Sector Agent is one of constant travel and danger at every turn."

"Oh, I wonder what that would be like." I nearly laughed at my own joke. My life was exactly that, only I was not authorized to brandish a weapon when danger appeared. I often did, but was not authorized to do so.

"But you travel with a repair vessel, surely it is an exciting life. I'll wager you see more danger than I do in some ports. But what brings you to Icarus?"

I side-stepped his comment, as lately there was danger at every turn. "I've come to connect with an old friend. And you?"

"The wedding, of course. I took time to see my friend married. He was an agent, but is leaving the unit for the life of a humble clerk with a wife at home."

"It sounds very sensible."

"How strange that we meet in a port unknown to either of us."

"Chance and Fate are twin sisters, I've heard."

"You're a poet as well as a philosopher," said the handsome Sector Agent named Honor.

"Toth. Isn't that a contraction of Thoth, from Earth mythology?"

"I suppose, if one is a student of such things. What is the origin of Souci?"

"It is a flower, the marigold, which holds a dual meaning, that of *presage* and *trouble*."

"And which are you, Souci?"

"A little of both, Honor. When trouble is around, it seems to find me, but quite often I see it coming."

A face flickered in the crowd, one I didn't recognize, yet knew. Not the face itself, but the type of face, of someone who had just found what he had been looking for. I had seen several such faces in the past and the events did not end calmly.

The man was tall and large. Of course, he could have been a guest. He could have been another Sector Agent; they tend to be muscular and bigger than most men.

"Are there many from your unit here at the wedding?" I asked, hoping for confirmation. Perhaps the man wasn't showing recognition at seeing me, but at seeing Honor Toth.

"No, I am the only one who made the trip. Why do you ask?"

"I thought I saw someone. He looked as if he might be a Sector Agent. He looked as if he recognized you."

"It might have been our mutual friend from the tavern on Ceres Segundo, but he's still in the cells. Where is this mystery man who has wrested your attention from me?"

I looked through the crowd, but didn't see him. It was not new to me that someone would see me through a crowd and then disappear. Usually, they reappear minutes later brandishing weapons.

Stranger at the Party

My inner guard went up and my muscles tightened having seen a stranger taking undue interest in me.

"Whoa, Miss Bach. Who is this fellow you saw? What's got you on point?" Honor was good; he spotted the hackles on my neck rise as I changed to a defensive stance.

"It's nothing, I'm sure. I'm overly cautious. Let's enjoy the wedding. Find me the girl with the fish, cheese and cracker snacks."

I took Honor's arm and walked through the crowd seeking the delicious delicacies, but also keeping a watchful eye for strangers I might know too well.

At the receiving line, I saw him again, the man who recognized me. He was behind the line, holding a comm unit to his ear, his back to the party.

How strange, I thought, *to live a life where mere recognition by another is cause for alarm. I started out so well. Where did I go wrong?*

"Honor, do you know that man?" I indicated the stranger on the phone. "Is he a friend of the groom or the bride?"

"I don't know him. I can ask. You're not going to leave me for him, are you?"

"No," I said, as if in a dream. Files of memories flooded my brain and I looked through them all for some familiar image, something to give a significance to the man who appeared at the party.

My response was an honest answer to the question, but Honor's silence made me turn to him. He was looking at me as if he didn't know what to expect.

"I mean, no, silly, of course not." I pulled my attention from old memories and strange men to playfully punched Honor in the mid-section, making him laugh.

"Good, I wouldn't want you to take off with a total..."

The man ended his conversation on the comm-link and turned around. One glance told me all I needed to know: his eyes targeted me.

He parted the reception line and charged at me like a wild animal, those eyes filled with unexplained hatred.

Honor released my arm and stepped in his way, his hands forming fists, preparing to remove this man from the waking world.

The man caught sight of Honor and formed a fist of his own. A giant left hand closed and aimed at Honor, promising to send him to the ground. Honor brought up his own left hand, only holding a small skillet from the food-prep table.

The stranger's fist hit the skillet with a resounding clang. The air was filled with the sound of several bones breaking. The stranger crumbled to the ground, howling and holding his broken hand.

When he stood up again, he had a blaster in his right hand and a wild look in his eye. He was aiming straight at me.

Honor pushed me out of the way. He picked up an empty serving tray from the nearest table and sailed it at the man. Without missing a beat, he charged the man, kicking the blaster from his hand.

Honor's push sent me further than he meant and I flew into a floating tray of Pruniers. The tightly wrapped delicacies made from the flowering prune tree signified *independence*, but had become a wedding favorite none-the-less.

Heads turned at the clatter as I fell over the floating tray, causing the magnetic balance to become disrupted and the tray to spill Pruniers over the nearby guests.

I was up in a flash, in time to see Honor strike the man in the face, sending his head spinning to the right. Teeth and blood flew across the lawn and into the fish pond. Girls screamed. A few of the men did as well.

The man reeled from Honor's blow but didn't go down. He came back with a flying tackle taking the Sector Agent down to the ground with him.

"Oooph!" Honor hit the ground. He came up fighting again, all feet and fists and in seconds was standing over the bleeding stranger. He struck the man once, twice, three times across the face and sent him rolling across the green and toward the fear-stricken wedding party.

The stranger stood up, bent with pain but with murder in his eyes. He had used the blows Honor had delivered to roll across the grass and recover his weapon. He raised blaster, targeting the Sector Agent, but then he spotted me.

Honor lunged at the stranger but too late. The man pointed his blaster directly at me and pulled the trigger. The blaster spat a tongue of blue flame as I dove out of its path.

The blast of blue fire struck the luncheon buffet vaporizing the large punch bowl and sending plates of rolled torpedoes in all directions. Bread and seasoned meats flew over the bride and groom in a spray.

My flight to avoid his blaster had sent me directly into the table holding the wedding cake. The table collapsed under the weight of the cake and me together. The nine-layer cake with white frosting, pink and blue trimming and topped with silken doves cushioned my fall nicely, covering me from head to toe in sugary goodness and fluffy white demon-food cake.

The stranger fired twice more, but not at me. This time the blue flames were intended to clear his path of the innocent gawkers who stood in his way as he ran from the garden.

Women screamed, falling into the arms of their men. The men fell back, catching their ladies but also pulling them away from the disturbance. Flowers were dropped in the confusion and were trampled underfoot by fleeing guests. Through the middle of the parting sea of color ran the madman in dark, sinister clothes and a blaster in his hand.

When the confusion settled, no one was hurt but the bride's wedding cake was completely destroyed. Everywhere, elegant, colorful women sat in the mud and cried as their gentlemen tried awkwardly to raise them up again. In the middle of the confusion I stood, under the gaze of a bewildered Sector Agent, covered in cake.

Getaway

"He got away," said Honor, reaching a hand to me.

"He'll be easy to spot, though. Tell the constables to look for a man with a black eye and a broken nose, covered in a flagon of blood and missing several teeth."

Honor pulled me to him. He looked at me, his face turned slightly to the side. He had dealt with fugitives his entire career and knew the signs.

"They'll want to talk with you."

"That's not a good idea," I told him. "After all, I wasn't really invited to the wedding."

"Let's get you cleaned and looking tidy. You know, in years to come, other couples will marvel at the story and wish they had a tale as exciting to tell."

"Yeah, let's come back when it's that time. Right now, I think I'm not only in the cake but in the soup as well. Perhaps I should leave now."

"Come this way."

Honor opened a door and guided me through it to a kitchen and staging area. He picked up a towel as we went and handed it to me. At the first staircase, we went down, winding around to the cellar.

"There's bound to be a refresh room down here. Take off your clothes."

"This is not how I hoped to hear you say that," I said, trying to lighten the mood as I searched through the cake for buttons.

"Not now. First we clean you up, and then we talk. If after that we're still on speaking terms, we'll discuss what you would like to hear me say." Agent Toth pushed me into the refresh room and closed the door.

Footsteps passed by the door and resonated above my head with what I knew to be the sensible shoes of the local constables.

Excited voices chattered and somewhere a girl was crying, occasionally screaming something profane. I knew the bride was off in a corner weeping for her perfect day. Her buffet table was

55

ruined, her guests were frightened and in the middle of it all, her cake was smashed by a girl she didn't even invite. When the constables asked, she no doubt tried to remember as much as possible about the girl who caused it all, the man with the gun and everyone screaming. She was a wreck! I only hoped she could get married in spite of everything and that her husband would take her for a long, restful honeymoon to the Wind Pools.

In the refresh room, I took off my skirt and blouse, ruined from the cake and icing, and washed myself off as best I could. I cleaned the cake from my blade and retied it around my thigh. Getting the cake out of my hair was the hardest part, once I had given up on my clothes.

A knock on the door made me turn, one hand on my blade handle.

"Souci! It's Honor. Open the door."

"It's open."

"You should have locked it," Honor said as he came in. He had a parcel over his arm wrapped in a table cover.

"Nobody's down here but us. They're all upstairs telling the police about the girl who crashed their party in the literal sense."

Honor looked at me. Without my skirt and blouse, I was wearing the standard dress for the Wind Pools, silk shorts and short top. The shorts were a size small, as was the top. There was more of me showing than I wanted in front of a man I hoped to impress, as close to naked as I wanted to get, unless he was going to talk a little kinder to me.

"Put this on. We're going to get out of here. We have to find a place where I can get the story straight."

"Am I under bond?" I asked, wondering where Honor stopped and Sector Agent Toth began.

"Do you need to be?" he replied.

"No, I'd rather not, if you don't mind."

"Then get dressed and come with me."

The dress was black and white, a uniform of sorts, no doubt brought for the kitchen workers. The black skirt attached to the white blouse and an apron went over the whole affair to indicate serving staff. Honor handed me the skirt and blouse, laying the apron aside. I put them on, careful not to look in the mirror. It didn't matter how I looked, it mattered how others viewed me. I turned to Honor and curtsied.

"What do you think, Sector Agent?"

"It will work. Let's go."

"Wait, wait, just one moment." I reached into my skirt pocket to retrieve my identochip. Honor saw the chip and his brows deepened. He looked from my eyes to my neck, to the scar just above my collar bone on the left. I could see the wheels turning. Was he mentally going through the local laws regarding chip removal? Was I one of those who proudly showed my scar, my emblem of freedom?

I hadn't tattooed around my scar as some had. Of course, mine wasn't from a chip, I never had one. The only identochip I wore in school was attached to my uniform with a security pin. No, my scar was given to me by my uncle as a going away present. I hid it whenever I could.

"This way," said Agent Toth, following his instincts. The Sector Agent was in charge now. Honor, the gentle man from the wedding, would be subdued until events evened out.

Through the dark, dank cellar, Agent Toth guided me along low corridors, past wine racks and storage rooms, to a flight of stairs winding upward. We came out in a spring house at the edge of the garden.

In the distance, constables were questioning the guests and the not-so-happy couple. The bride was indeed crying about her cake.

"Some bumps and bruises, but no one hurt."

"That's good. Please believe me, if I had known..."

"Yes, Souci, I know. Keep going, please."

Agent Toth guided me out of the garden and down the avenue in the same direction I had been walking earlier. The airship had emptied its passengers, loaded another batch and was just lifting up for its run around the bay.

Interrogation

At a cafe, Agent Toth guided me to a booth at the rear, as far from the door as possible.

"Uh, we're not open sir," began the boy wiping tables.

"Sector Agent. Official business. We don't want to be bothered." Agent Toth produced his identification and flashed it for the boy, who backed down immediately. He returned to his task with his head down.

"Now! Who is the man with the blaster?" began Toth.

"I don't know. I have never seen him before. I don't know his name and can only guess at his motivation."

"Then guess."

I looked into his eyes, cold and gray, wishing I could be anywhere but in the cafe booth being interrogated by a man I'd prefer to kiss. In dreams, I wanted to meet him again. Now we were at a cafe booth and he expected me to talk and make sense at the same time. It was not what I had in mind, but it's what I had to deal with.

"My father left me an inheritance. There was some money early on, but my uncle spent most of it. The rest went to schooling. Later I found more he had tucked away and bought my ship, which is in port waiting for me. I should contact her."

"Your ship," echoed Toth.

"Yes."

"Go on."

"Over the course of time, there have been men, and a woman, people who thought it would be easier to steal my inheritance than to work. They were mistaken. I'm guessing he's the latest in a long line of thieves."

"You think he was out to steal your fortune."

"It seems likely, my fortune or perceived fortune. It's one explanation."

"How did he know you were here?"

"Now that is a mystery. There is only my vessel who knows we are on this planet, my crew who knows which way I began to walk and no one at all who knew I was at the wedding. I'm sorry about the cake."

"Never mind the cake. Who is your crew?"

"Chineel is my first mate, she's also a good friend and would never betray me. Dagon is my second mate and my protector. He would do anything to protect me. Flax is the vessel..."

"Your vessel is named Vax?"

"Flax, the flower signifying *benefactor*. She is my benefactor, so I named her Flax."

"Your ship." Agent Toth was clearly not getting the relationship I had with my vessel.

"That's right, Sector Agent Toth, and if you are lucky enough to meet her, you will understand. She is my ally and best friend." I lowered my voice: "Take that tone again, Sector Agent, and you will find me a difficult subject for conversation."

"Fair enough. Who are you?"

I looked at the Agent. He wanted an answer and he didn't want to hear a "shore story." It was time to come clean and to a Sector Agent. My pause was taken as reluctance, so he continued.

"At first, I thought you were a stowaway, as you were aboard an automated vehicle. They don't usually have passengers or crew. I was surprised you didn't jump at my offer. A position with the Agents is prized."

"At the time, I was in search of my inheritance."

"So who are you? You're not Souci Bach. I didn't believe that when you first said it."

"Well, I am, in many ports. Who you are depends on where you are these days. On Khons, where I am from, I'm Starwort Bacchus, daughter of Doctors Mister and Mrs. Bacchus, now deceased. Take me to the Wind Pools and they will welcome me as Miss Souci Bach. I've not been in the world long, but there are places where the name Starwort raises an eyebrow. In those places, Souci Bach walks freely."

The Sector Agent looked at me unchanged. We stared at each other for a moment, and then he looked away. He turned back to me and twisted his mouth to one side, then blew out a gust of air.

"What are you doing here on Cecrops?"

"I came to find a friend. He's a little ragged, but is a good man. His last coordinates were here but when we arrived, he was not at home. We think he had not been home for longer than it takes to make a trip to the corner cafe."

"So you think he's run off?"

"Or been taken. I was looking for anything to give me a lead when I got swept up by a wedding party. You may remember it."

"Your friend's name?"

"Galium."

Agent Toth's face didn't change, but there was a near imperceptible quiver in his lip. He recognized the name.

"Galium. Galium is your friend. Galium, the most sought-after radical activist on the outer rim. Galium with no less than a dozen warrants in his name to be taken under bond. Galium who has been critical of the Central Government since the rise of Seb to power."

"So sorry, but I don't know the name, Seb."

"Seb, the President of the Central Government on Earth. Only one man opposes him: one called Galium."

"Yes, Galium. We met in the low islands of New Babylon. We used to discuss Paganism in the New Age and write poetry. More recently, he told me about the Grecian Flu and the spread of the Central Government."

"There's no connection there."

"I know more than you do, Agent. He also told me about the nanochips embedded in tattoo ink for those who have removed their chips and tattoo around the scar as a statement."

"Is that how you got your scar?" Agent Toth pointed at my neck, at the scar I wore there. It was usually covered, but my hair was wet and not behaving.

"No, my uncle gave me that. I wasn't compliant enough. He was not very nice."

"Where is he now?"

"Lying still in a tiny porcelain canister in a landfill."

"So, dead."

"Or very uncomfortable."

The staring match continued. Agent Toth tapped a pinky finger on the edge of the table while he regarded me with the knowledgeable glare of a Sector Agent.

"What do you want with Galium?"

"To know he's all right. If I find him and he tells me to get lost, that he's fine, I'll fly back to my planet."

"Khons?"

"Bacchus. My father left me a planet."

Toth's eyebrows went up. He apparently had never heard of someone being given a planet before.

"So you didn't find Galium."

65

"No."

"I'm walking you back to your vessel. I want you to stay on it until I find out what I can about this man who crashed the party and about your friend, Galium."

"So, I'm not under bond?"

"No, but you should be. For now, I just want you safe."

Agent Toth stood up and motioned me to the door. Outside, the traffic was picking up for the mid-day rush. It looked to me as if everyone in Icarus wanted to be somewhere else and in a hurry.

Mis-step

Datur Minot was furious. He stormed across the office in front of a bank of windows, his hands in the air and delivered his message at the top of his lungs.

"You fired a blaster in the middle of a wedding party, lost your target and attracted the attention of a Sector Agent," yelled Datur.

"I didn't know there were Sector Agents," replied Hephae. He regarded Datur from beneath lowered brows. Hephae hated explaining himself, especially to a lesser man, like Datur Minot.

"The only thing you did right was to not kill Starwort Bacchus. Do you think she can tell us how to access what we seek if she is dead?"

"She had help. A Sector Agent..."

"Yes, I know, I know. I saw the whole thing."

"Saw?"

"Of course. Did you think I would let you out of my sight? I had a hover-drone following the whole time."

"You were watching me?" Hephae said, raising his voice to express his displeasure at being spied upon.

"How do you think I stay one step ahead of this infernal girl? I watch everything, I listen to everything, I know everything." Datur punctuated his sentence with a finger to his head.

"I had her, but there were too many people, oh, and a Sector Agent," shouted Hephae. "Did I mention the Sector Agent?"

"Give me the blaster. You're not supposed to kill this girl; you're supposed to subdue her and bring her in."

"How am I supposed to do that?"

"She'll return to the garden; she has a misplaced sense of honesty and will bring the uniform back. When she does, you'll be waiting. You will handle the girl with a gentle hand, so she will be alive to tell us what we need to know."

"And then we're done."

Datur darkened. He glared at Hephae, who was already looking for an exit door. People who want the job to be over before it begins always put Datur on edge.

"The girl is with the Sector Agent for now. Get a good night's sleep and we'll begin again in the morning."

"Why can't I..." Hephae said, reaching for his blaster.

"Please don't make me regret hiring you so early in our relationship, Mr. Hephae. Do as you're told."

Hephae sighed and sulked out of the office.

Datur watched the mercenary leave.

"Why do I have to work with such cretins?" he asked aloud, of no one in particular.

"Because they are the only sort who will do the work," said a sultry voice behind him.

A woman stepped from the inner office, tall and statuesque with classic features framed in soft billows of strawberry blond hair. She boasted strong shoulders with long arms and graceful hands. Her waist narrowed and then flared to hips as wide as her shoulders. Over this was stretched a dress of deep red silk, cut low at the bust to reveal her ample cleavage and up to the thigh at the hem, revealing long sensuous legs.

Crinole Gorgon, named for the Crinole flower, signifying *delicate weakness*, was anything but delicate or weak. She dressed to convey sexual desire, though it was the last thing on her mind. She dressed that way to put men off their guard and under her control. She had discovered it to work in every situation so far. This one was no different.

She walked over to Datur's desk and placed a reassuring hand on his shoulder.

"When we have the girl, you will extract from her all we need to know. Then you can give her to the cretin. I'm certain he already has plans for her."

"I didn't want to offer him that much. Forty percent is more than I am prepared to part with."

"Do you really believe he will see any part of it? We are not putting a pile of money on the table and dividing it into stacks. There is much more to consider than mere money, much more."

"The deeds will have to be considered, and how to best make use of her planet. There is no telling if it is habitable. Is it of any value?"

"There are other considerations closer to hand."

"Other than her family inheritance?"

"Two technologies, Mister Minot. Starwort Bacchus has access to two technologies and never thinks about them. She has in her possession a pin given to her by Doctor Aristaeus Genus, creator of many of the devices we use every day. She is friends with Genus and through her we can get to him. His new innovations will be next year's production models."

"Doctor Genus engineered a cloaking device; I have seen the first generation prototype."

"He has taken it further. Miss Bacchus has a later version in the form of a pin. When she wears it, she is invisible to surveillance units of all sorts, even yours. But there is another prize to be had, one that surpasses all that went before."

"What is that, Miss Gorgon?"

"Her ship, Mister Minot. Her ship is the prize."

Reports

"Weekly reports, Sir," Sergeant Phaeton said with a snap. He placed the metallic blue stick on the desk of Captain Vikare. There was nothing outstanding or urgent in the report, nothing to spur the Icarus Constable Force on Cecrops to action. It was a typical quiet day in the tourist haven of Icarus.

"Thank you, Sergeant. Anything of note?"

"Three reports of interest, Captain. Two of them months old, all from Copernicus."

"Copernicus!" the Captain spat. "Always good for a juicy report. What is it now? Or should I say, what was it then?"

"Ha! Good one, Sir. Well, Adox Willamette was taken, charged and put in high security, but he was so thoroughly stung by Malameris tentacles during the course of his arrest, he never made it to see a judge."

The captain picked up his power ale, took a long, slow sip and replaced it on his desk coaster. He knew the name, of course. What constable didn't?

"Who will we chase, now that Adox is gone? What else, Sergeant?"

"Grantham Dodd, confidence man and swindler, found dead in a speeder crash on the coast road. Took them this long to identify the body. Another speeder fell on him and the joint explosion - well, sir, you know."

"Killed him? Yes, Speeder core explosions will do that. He'll be missed. I loved investigating Dodd. Always pretty women around Dodd. Was he doing the chasing or being chased?"

"Sir?" said the sergeant, looking up from the readout hovering over the reader/scanner.

"You said two speeders but didn't mention a second body. Coast road, not a place for a speeder under normal circumstances, so one must assume a chase. Was there a second body?"

"No, sir. Nothing here about a second body.

"Someone got away. Any idea who?"

"No, sir. There's nothing more in the file."

"Mm-hmm! What's the third thing you said?"

"Datur Minot, Sir. He's popped up again."

Captain Vikare became very animated all at once. He sat up, looked at the sergeant and fired a verbal missile.

"What? You should have led with that, Sergeant! The rest would have been unnecessary. Show me the report. Where is he? What is he up to? What have you got?"

The sergeant sprang into action, poking fingers at the air to activate buttons only visible to direct sight, bringing up the report he mentioned, complete with full details.

"Uh, Datur Minot: Wanted for technical espionage, privacy invasion and breach of government security. It goes on from there, more of the same."

"Yes, and that's just to start. He's been linked to more than three dozen rings, said to be the brains behind some of the biggest breaches in security throughout the middle planets. I wonder if he had anything to do with Dodd's death. Or Willamette's death, for that matter?"

"I doubt it, Sir. What could he be doing associating with those two? Now that I think of it, what would they be doing associating with each other?"

"Together they escaped from a level six security facility, Sergeant. That seems a good enough platform for a business relationship, don't you think?"

"Yes, Sir. I suppose it does. But for Minot to become associated with men of that sort..."

The Sergeant seemed to hang in mid-air for an instant, then began poking at the air again.

"Wait, there was something in the last report about a man under surveillance in Copernicus who slipped his shadows. He is whereabouts unknown. Goes by the single name of Hephae. Do you think there's something in the wind?"

"Could be, Sergeant. I want everything on my desk as soon as possible, everything you've got on this Hephae, on Minot, the two dead men and anything that looks suspicious. Click, click, click! Get to it!"

The sergeant left, in a hurry for the first time all day, leaving Captain Vikare to ponder accidents, mistakes and coincidences. Of course, he knew there were mistakes. Promoting Officer Phaeton to Sergeant was one, he would remind himself daily. But there were no accidents, no coincidences. Everything was connected.

"Printouts, Phaeton!" yelled the captain. "I like printouts."

"Yes, sir!" the sergeant shouted from the hallway.

Within minutes, three more metallic blue sticks appeared on the desk and a stack of thin plastic sheets, each the size of a folio. The captain shuffled the plastic sheets and laid them out on the desk until they were in an order he liked. He looked them over and smiled like a hungry man set before a meal.

"Aha! Yes, Minot returns to Daedalus. At the same time, a criminal of interest goes missing in Copernicus. Sergeant, I want you to give me a listing of all vessels leaving Copernicus since the time of the speeder crash and all vessels arriving recently on Cecrops. Next, I'll have all wants and alerts from any location where Dodd's name or Willamette's name crops up. Find me a connection of Minot to Dodd. There's something interesting going on. This might turn out to be a good day after all."

Introductions

Sector Agent Honor Toth escorted me to the skyport where Flax sat waiting. While I was sure she saw us coming, I made a show of walking up to the port bay door and announcing myself.

"Captain Bacchus and guest, requesting entrance."

Without hesitation, the door opened. I could smell stew cooking inside. A glance around the bay told me I had nothing to worry about with regard to guests arriving, the house was tidy.

Chineel and Dagon had just returned having found no hint of where Galium might have gone. It wasn't quite time for the evening meal, but it was close enough for Chineel to be in the galley making pleasing noises with pottery. She had a stew on a low cook pad.

Honor walked into the bay and looked around, prepared to make a judgment. He nodded his head, his mouth twisted off to the right. He approved.

"Come meet the crew," I said as I pulled him toward the galley.

Chineel's expression changed to that of a vixen temptress as she saw the handsome man enter and prepared to steal him away. I moved to cut her off.

"Relax, lady, I saw him first. Honor, this is Chineel. The desperado at the end of the table is Dagon. He is invaluable."

"How?"

"Hmm?"

"How is he invaluable?"

"Dagon is my bodyguard. He protects me."

Dagon smiled, self-assured as usual. He crossed his arms and looked dangerous for the Agent.

"Chineel, Dagon, this is Honor Toth, Sector Agent. You've heard me tell of the handsome Sector Agent of Ceres; here he is in the flesh."

"Agent," Chineel said, blushing like a young bride.

At the table, Dagon stood, pulling himself up to full height, ready to defend his captain if needed.

"Hello, Chineel, Dagon. I've heard good things about both of you. And about your vessel. Hello Flax," he added, looking around the galley.

"Hello, Agent Toth," Flax said from the galley console.

Honor jumped, not expecting a reply. The voice came from the holographic likeness Doctor Genus had given to Flax at our last stop to Victoriana.

"Oh! You weren't kidding, very much a 'she.' Hello, Flax, it's a pleasure to meet you."

"Thank you, Agent. And thank you for keeping our captain safe. The reports of a madman running rampant through a wedding were both disturbing and illuminating."

"What?" cried Dagon and Chineel in tandem.

"It was nothing, but I did fall into the cake."

Flax smiled as Dagon and Chineel noted my dress for the first time, the black and white attire of a serving hostess.

"Where's your skirt and blouse?" asked Chineel.

"Tucked under a table in the preparation room at the Garden Pavilion on Portside. It took me a while to wash the cake from my hair."

"Was it good?" asked Chineel, poking fun.

"Delicious. I only wish the bride and groom had been able to enjoy it."

"You were never one for a nice, quiet party. Anyone hungry for stew?"

We were all ready for stew, save for Flax, who didn't excuse herself, she just closed her eyes and faded away. There were perimeters to check and other safeguards to see to. All the rest could wait; her captain had a guest.

The supper was interrupted by an alarm, a constant beeping from the bay that chased thoughts of hot stew from my thoughts. All four of us ran to the bay. The alarm was from the bay door. Someone had tried to open the door from the outside without clearance.

"Intruder alert, Captain. There has been an attempt to tamper with the port bay door. Here is a likeness of the intruder."

At the bay console, a recording of a man at the door, failing to gain entry and then running away played, paused and repeated. It was the man who had chased us through the wedding party.

"That's the man who ruined the wedding," Honor said to my crew.

"Thank you, Honor. For a moment there I thought you were going to say the man who made me ruin it."

"It was the blaster that made the difference. You're much too graceful to fall into a cake unless you're dodging a deadly blast."

Flax appeared in her holographic splendor.

"I knew there was something, Captain. I've been feeling it since we first entered Cecrops air space. There has been someone tapping in to our signal."

"Can you tell who, Flax? Might it be Galium?"

"No, Captain, not Galium. Galium's signal is unique. This one is like a thousand others, so much so that it might be considered an accident, but it is the same accident over and over. That's not an accident, that's invasion."

"You're right, Flax. I believe the culprit will be whoever is guiding the man who attacked your captain at the wedding."

I knew at once he was right. Before I could fully form the thought in my head, I blurted it out for all.

"There seems to be an unlimited supply of bad guys who find me immensely interesting. I wonder why."

Daybreak

We buttoned Flax up for the night and shuttled to a secure spot on the skyport. Sector Agent Toth returned to his hotel to face his friend the groom and comfort the bride after the disaster her wedding had become. I didn't want that duty and wished him well.

Sleep didn't come easily, but when it did, it was complete. When I awoke, it was several hours later. There had been no dreams during the night, only sleep. The changed readout on the console being my only confirmation.

I awoke and dressed in my heavy unitard, more suited to a chilly morning. I rolled the wait-staff uniform in a bundle and slipped out of the port bay onto the chilly deck of the skyport. It was a long walk into town, but if I timed it right, I could return the dress and retrieve my skirt and blouse before anyone discovered them and checked for my identifying trace.

It was still dark when I reached the edge of town. More than once I questioned the sanity of my quest, but once begun, I had no choice but to go on.

The only vehicles out were the slow-moving trash barges, creeping inches above the ground, hovering from bin to bin in a carefully prearranged pattern. I counted seventeen such levitating lorries by the time I reached the Garden Pavilion. Each bore a central compartment and two mechanical arms which lifted refuse bins from the left and the right, and then dumped their contents rudely into its belly.

The gate to the garden was locked, but it was little effort to scale the side trellis and pop over the wall. The garden had been cleared in preparation for the morning setup and the next wedding party. It was hoped no one would shoot into the gathered guests or fall into the cake.

In the changing area, I returned the server's uniform to the rack of similar outfits ready for the next day's staff. From under a table, I retrieved my skirt and blouse, rolled them together in a hurried bundle and tucked them into a bundle preparing to return the same way I came.

"Someone's in here," said a man's voice.

I froze.

"Is someone in here?" said another voice, higher and softer than the first, a woman.

"I heard someone in the back," said the first voice.

"You're imagining things, Horace, there's no one here. Just get your uniform and let's get started."

"I could have sworn..." the voices faded.

The tell-tale whine of a floating refuse barge lifting a bin over its head covered the rest of the conversation. I heard the crashing of assorted trash emptying into the main container. The reaching arm banged the bin several times to make sure it was empty before returning it to the alley-side refuse area. I crept to the side door and peeked out. The barge was moving down the alley to the next pickup spot. The operator rode on a special platform at the rear, designed to keep him at the switch rather than walking back and forth to and from the controls in the front cab.

As I slipped through the side door to the access road, a figure at the other end of the road turned around in the shadows. He took a sudden interest in my end of the alley and began walking toward me, still in the shadows against the brick wall. I turned away from him and walked down the alleyway toward the trash barge as it lumbered down the lane, lifting each bin and returning it to its previous spot. The footsteps behind me quickened.

Halfway to the land-barge, I broke into a run. the footsteps behind me did the same, removing all doubt about the agenda of the man behind me. Ahead, the barge took up nearly the entire alley. Getting around it could be difficult. If I stop to squeeze by, the man behind me could catch up and grab me.

Written across the rear, faded yet legible, was "Icarus Refuse Collection." The man on the rear platform moved the barge forward. In the side mirror, I could see there was no one in the cab.

At the side of the IRC barge, the running footsteps behind me were catching up; I couldn't outrun this man. At the open barge door, I climbed inside the cab. In the right-side mirror, I saw the driver step off the platform to arrange a bin that had been returned off-center to its slot. The arm was retracted while the driver secured the bin.

Below me, a switch said "Left Retriever" in red. I pulled that lever and the left-side arm unfolded from the side of the body and lowered. The running man ran into the lowered arm, smashing his face. He reeled and staggered back, holding the brickwork for support.

I knew he wouldn't be distracted for long and I knew there was no place to run where I could get away. The clear readout hovering over the console was similar to a land barge I had driven on Sterope. Remembering the sequence, I tapped the dots to shift into primary gear and felt the great barge move forward.

In the mirror, I saw the driver chasing me down the alley. In the other side mirror, the man from the alley picked himself up and began to follow me, though slower than he had before. I shifted to the secondary gear and left both men behind.

In the early morning hours the refuse removal vehicles had the run of the road. The streets were empty, too early for business traffic. The transport lumbered forward into the street on giant hoverpads the size and speed of an elephant's foot.

Odd that such a leisurely pace would still require split-second decisions, but they had to be made. I had no idea where I was or what was around me, so I turned right for no reason.

In the mirror, I saw the man exit the alley running toward me with increasing speed. In the growing light of morning and out of the shadow of the alley, I saw his face: It was the same man who fired at me during the wedding; the same man who tried to break into the bay doors on the skyport.

Elephant Chase

My mind went into overdrive as I considered my options. I had my small blade, but it might not be much of a weapon against a man of his size. I had left the comm behind, thinking I would return within minutes. Run, fight, hide. All seemed pointless; my options were few.

The whirring sound and the gauge told me I had reached the height of the mechanical gear and had to find the next higher gear. Up ahead, the road turned, with a cafe directly ahead. If I didn't take the turn, I would plunge the truck into the cafe. I had no choice but to take the turn.

Rather than risk the higher gear, I stayed in the secondary and tapped the foot lever for the brake. I risked being caught by the running man, but at least I wouldn't overturn the vehicle or crash into the cafe.

As the barge tilted into the curve, hovermags on the left side lifted too far from the road, losing traction. I could feel the contents of the half-filled refuse-bay shifting as the vehicle leaned. The city's trash went first to localized compactors, then to the collectors for a trip to the land-fill zone out of town. The compacted garbage was dense and heavy, giving heft to the vehicle and hindering speed and maneuverability.

Coming out of the turn, I stepped on the accelerator and the secondary gear whined louder. I straightened out and struggled for third gear with one eye on the mirror for the man chasing me and one eye on the alley coming up on the right.

A similar refuse collection vehicle emerged at a snail's pace from the alleyway, stopping at the road as if listening for the sound of approaching traffic. We missed crashing into each other by an arm's length. As I drifted by, in a gear rarely used by land barges, I could see the surprised face of the driver.

The road before me was empty of traffic. The day was overcast and told lies concerning the arrival of dawn, as there was no sun to be had. The cloud cover could have worked for me or against me, I wasn't sure.

In the side mirror, I saw the running man open the door to the other land barge, pull the driver out and fling him onto the street. The driver rolled twice and scurried to the curb on his hands and knees, eager to get out of the way of the madman who was stealing his refuse collector. The running man brought the barge out onto the street, the gears and pulleys whining as he overextended the mechanisms.

A smile came unbidden to my lips. He had no experience with larger vehicles, whereas I had driven a land barge. One five-minute experience beats none. I was points ahead. But I was still in a chase.

Another mandatory turn approached and I shifted down to take it without crashing into the houses on the far side. Old-style lanterns lined the roadside like trees, spaced out with thirty feet between them. As I hovered by, they snuffed out with the coming of the day. In the mirror, I saw the chasing barge knock three of them to the ground as it went by. The three minor crashes punctuated the turn but he kept coming. In the windscreen, the face of the following man was fierce and determined.

He's not just doing a job, I thought. *He's angry on top of it. What did I ever do to him? Except not die, of course. For some, that's enough.*

The visiting circus at Sterope came into my mind. The sluggish, measured pace of the mammoths leading the town parade made an impression on me, lumbering along, deliberate and in slow-motion. There was no hurrying these great beasts, and there was no stopping them. If they chose to go into the crowd, anyone in their path would be trampled underfoot.

Today felt similar, caught up in a chase comprised of the slow moving vehicles of the Icarus Refuse Collection department. The measured lumbering of the mechanical behemoths was overly predictable. I even had tusks.

"Tusks?" I said, looking up over the cab. There were two long, pointed bars of metal bouncing along over me. On the console, a collection of work-worn levers caused me to divide my attention between the road and the controls. "Which one? Which one?"

I chose one that looked likely and pulled it. The rig in front dropped as huge pistons at the side of the vehicle activated, pulling the two straight tusks down to street level. I returned the lever and watched the tusks move upward, back to the top of the vehicle.

"Good to know."

A glance in the rear mirror told me I had tarried too long playing with the fork-lift. The other trash collector was gaining on me. The face of the man driving it grew larger and more menacing as he gritted his teeth. His eyes blazed with red-hot anger.

Why do these guys always have to make it personal? I asked myself. I didn't even know this man and he was trying to kill me.

The other hover-barge came at me full-force, at a reckless speed, drifting like a parade float decorated in garbage. The barge drifted toward me, unable to stop or be deterred. I couldn't speed up, turn away or otherwise avoid him. All I could do was to grit my teeth and get ready for a pounding.

He bumped the left-rear quadrant of my vehicle with his right-front protector. I drifted into a building to my right, unable to do otherwise. The crash occurred in slow motion with pieces of brick and plasticast crumbling onto the pavement. The right window and windscreen cracked and splintered.

I rebounded onto the street and into the other hover barge, sending him in turn into several parked speeders, usually out of the way enough to avoid damage, but not today. Today there were garbage barges smashing into one another like slow bouncy-cars at the fairgrounds.

He recovered from the smashed speeders and aimed at me once again, but he had lost speed and trajectory. Unable to gain traction to turn the lumbering beast in time, he headed into a stone wall. He struck it hard, sending pieces of stone in all directions and bouncing his vehicle back into the street in a slow spin. He ended his revolutions facing away from me and had to recover direction as well as momentum.

As he turned the barge in the street, lining it up for another run at me, I used the opportunity to put some distance between us.

The road ahead gave no exits and twisted this way and that; he had no choice but to follow. A curve came up, putting me temporarily out of his sight. This was my chance.

I downshifted to the secondary gear, stood on the brake treadle and turned sharply to the right, counting on a grid system I hoped was in place. The street was narrow and I couldn't help vaulting down its length bouncing from side to side. At the next right, I turned again. The street was wider, but my turn took too much room to make. The far side of the curve caused me to crash into a cafe window. At the next corner I had the same bad luck, taking out two kiosks, closed luckily, as it was too early for them to be open.

As I returned to the road I had just left, the IRC chase had reversed; I was behind the other trash barge.

A thrill came over me and I had to control myself to avoid overconfidence. I might have been able to turn a corner in this beast, but actually winning this race was out of the question. I had to get clever.

Chase's End

My heavy-footed chase vehicle lumbered toward the back of the ponderous barge ahead. As I drew closer, I dropped the giant fork on the front of the truck to the lower position, hoping I didn't come across a steep dip in the road; at this speed, I would flip the whole beast, sending me through the windscreen.

Inches away from the lead barge the man looked into his mirror and saw me. Shock spread across his features. He had been too busy looking for where I had gone to notice I was behind him. Now he was short on options and I was coming fast.

I guessed the distance from the back edge of the truck to the hoverpads, making sure the tips of the metal tusks were under the rear of his vehicle. Once sure they were not touching the hoverpads, I activated the lift. The back end of his barge raised off the road as mine dipped in front with the weight. The lifted barge shifted on the metal fork and slammed into the front of mine.

The hit jarred me. Cracks appeared in the glass.

I raised the fork higher, lifting the other barge beyond the capacity of the hoverpads. The front plate caught on the paving and his barge flipped over in a slow ballet, as if my elephant had given the other a lift and a push, allowing for a graceful, leisurely tumble to a perfect landing on point.

The toppled barge spilled its load onto the roadway and plopped upside-down onto the pile of stinking refuse. The cubes of compacted garbage separated, spilling ill-smelling bits of gooey stuff in every direction. The vehicle continued forward on a bed of garbage, skidding along the roadway sending sparks out to the sides as the metal ground against the stonework.

The rounded back rocked to and fro on the roadway; the weight of the truck sought to crush the cab a little at a time. The door flung open, kicked by a desperate foot. I saw the man leap out and cling to the sides of the open doorway, trying to escape the cab before it was crushed flat.

The trash barge continued to skid along the roadway upside-down and backwards with the cab in the rear, carried along by the sheer weight of the vehicle and collected garbage. Anything in its path was sure to be destroyed completely, not quickly, but at a tedious rate as the barge bounced along, with the driver hanging onto the doorway for his life.

I urged my barge forward, pushing the metal tusks through the windscreen and pulled the lever to lift the vehicle again.

The man leaped from the cab and rolled onto the roadway, crying out in pain as he hit the stones. I stopped and lowered the tusk assembly, dropping his vehicle to the road with a crash. I tapped in the reverse mode and pulled back from the demolished land barge, then turned into the lane to the left and away from the scene of the destruction, leaving the man who sought to kill me helpless in the roadway.

At the turn, the sound of sirens caught my attention. There would be constables in the chase soon and a decision would have to be made.

As the sirens surrounded me, rising and falling, though barely heard over the noise of the land barge, I slowed my pace. Several constabulary speeders passed me on the main thoroughfare as I rumbled toward the garden.

Several roadways beckoned me, each one looking familiar, each one promising a quick route back to the skyport and safety. Each promise of an escape route proved a lie as I rambled through the back lanes of Icarus.

At last, I saw a familiar sight. The garden loomed ahead, with the lights of a dozen constabulary speeders surrounding it.

Off to the side, three similar refuse barges sat silent as the drivers gathered by the intersection discussing what had occurred. I pulled my own next to theirs and alighted, my rolled skirt and blouse under my arm.

There was no activity behind the gardens, so with all the constables out front dealing with the gathering crowd, I walked unseen back to the skyport and through the port bay door. I had escaped and returned victorious.

"Are you all right, Star?"

"Yes, Flax. Thank you for asking. Is everyone still asleep?"

"Dagon, although I cannot see how, considering the noise outside. Did you see what is causing the disturbance?"

"Yes, Flax. It's me, I'm afraid. But I'm all right now."

"Chineel is in the galley. Cross to the starboard side and enter through your cabin if you like."

"Yes, Flax, thank you. That's a good idea."

I dropped my clothing on the bunk and slipped into my pajamas. I tousled my hair and prepared to meet the day. As I exited the Captain's quarters, I stretched.

"Breakfast, sleepy-head?" asked Chineel.

I walked into the galley wearing the hair style of a mad woman. I yawned broadly and flopped into a seat at the main table. "Whatever you have will be just fine."

"Coming right up. We have no new information concerning Galium."

"So, no change from last night?"

"No, no change. Nothing new. All the same."

"Hmm." I accepted a cup of morning ale from Chineel and rested my head in my hands.

Soon, I thought, the report of a mentally disturbed woman who stole a trash-collection hover-barge and engaged in an early morning chase with another will come over the air and my friends will turn their heads to me with questions in their eyes. Until then, I would wear a cloak of innocence; no one will know it was me behaving badly on the streets of Icarus.

The IEMC

Datur Minot stood at the receiving desk of the Icarus Emergency Medical Center with the look of one who is the father of an idiot son.

He had chosen Hephae out of two dozen potential recruits. The man had speed, strength and, so Datur thought, brains. He could shoot straight, use a knife well and could pick a pocket with the best. In the past, Hephae had retrieved plans from highly secure facilities and had been a collector for the black market drug consortium on Serapis.

Now Hephae was in the medical center with no foreseeable date for release and held under bond by constables. The nurse broke the news to Datur with a grim expression.

"I am sorry, but your friend has sustained two broken legs, fractures to his right arm in three places, a severe concussion and four broken ribs. He is not likely to be released soon. Besides, the Icarus Constabulary has him in manacles. He is reported to have stolen a city vehicle and crashed it, though how he was able to do that is unclear."

"He's a very capable man. I'm not surprised."

The nurse's expression said she didn't understand, but she nodded anyway. Datur rolled his eyes and left the front desk to find the exit; he had to get back to his office; he had a new boss and she wanted a report.

He had hoped to hire Crinole Gorgon to coax information out of Miss Bacchus once she had been brought in. It was a perfect plan: He would find the girl, Hephae would abduct her and bring her into the office. Then Miss Gorgon would get the information from her.

Instead, the woman had taken over. He thought he could handle her, but he could not. She had a cruel streak with no boundaries and a droid assistant with blast capabilities. If he didn't do as told, the droid would simply lift a finger and he would feel the pain from his little bald head to his out-sized feet.

Datur shook just to think of her. His hatred was beyond his ability to express. He could still hear the sentence that put the hat on the other head.

"You have an interesting operation here, Minot, but you are clearly not a leader. You lack direction and planning. I'll take it from here. Await instructions, that is, unless you wish to take it up with my assistant."

Ortie was a shorter version of Crinole Gorgon, but with a link to the city power core. One touch from her shining alloy hand and he would be fried, a charred bit of carbon ex-life-form.

No, he didn't want to take it up with her assistant. He wanted to go back in time before he ever met her and live that day over making different decisions.

Datur would have to be more clever if he wanted to survive this most recent mishap. Gorgon would not put up with another embarrassing disaster. Hephae had clearly become a liability and would have to be removed.

The only remaining item on the list was to ensure no link between Hephae and Datur Minot. If he could in any way be linked back to Datur, the authorities would be looking where they should not.

That meant Hephae would have to be removed quietly.

"It seems, Miss Gorgon, that we have lost an associate," Datur said when he returned to his office.

"Mister Hephae will no longer be with us, then? You will find a way to dispose of him, I trust."

"You never cared for him, did you, Miss Gorgon?"

"He lacked finesse."

Cautioned

"Bang! Bang! Bang!" interrupted breakfast.

"Constables!" said Chineel. She wore an apron tied over her sleepwear. Her hair was pinned up to get it out of her eyes, but not for meeting company and certainly not for an arrest photograph.

"How do you know?" Dagon asked.

"Constables always knock three times."

"Flax," I whispered, knowing she was never far.

Flax's holographic head appeared above the console unit against the wall. She appeared to be thinking.

"The man who was here with you yesterday is at the bay door seeking entrance. Shall I open the door for him?"

"Yes, Flax. Let him in. He won't go away, so might as well." I cupped my hot morning ale with both hands and put my bare feet on the seat next to me.

Sector Agent Honor Toth burst into the galley like a man on a mission. He was wide eyed, punctuating his tirade with percussive hand gestures.

"What do you think you are doing? Are you insane? That man is a killer! He's got a long history of violent offenses. Even without the charges being brought locally, Icarus Constabulary could take him under bond for a dozen outstanding warrants."

"What are you talking about? What man?"

"Don't do that; you know what man. He's a killer. Yes, I know, you're a Space Captain, but don't you know the danger you put yourself in?"

"Really, Agent, I don't..."

"Stop! Just stop! You know perfectly well what I'm talking about. You were described, and your skirt and blouse are missing."

Dagon's eyebrows went up as he looked from the agent to his captain with wonder. Chineel smiled, hoping to hear more about the missing skirt and blouse. The agent continued his broadside.

"Stop dodging! You're found out! How can you take such chances? What would I do if something happened to you?" he pleaded.

The galley was still. No one moved. From the console, Flax watched expectantly. Chineel stood motionless at the food prep counter waiting for whatever would come next to deny or confirm what the agent's last question inferred. Dagon raised his brows and his eyes grew wider. He was in uncharted territory.

I took a deep breath and let it out. There were cats out of bags all over the galley and no one able to return the status quo.

"I went to return the wait-staff uniform and to retrieve my own clothing. I had no idea he would be skulking in the shadows. I had little choice."

"But to steal a refuse barge?"

"I've driven a land barge before. It was as a toy in my hands."

"You perpetrated a high-speed chase through the streets of metropolitan Icarus."

"Hardly at high-speeds and certainly not metropolitan. They were hover barges, garbage trucks, there's only one thing slower and that's..." I couldn't remember the name. "Chineel, what was that moon-to-moon shuttle craft you turned into a house in Sterope? What was that called?"

"Never mind what it's called!" the Sector Agent yelled. "The point is, there is a wrecked city vehicle!

There is a man under arrest who will give your name! There is a warrant out for whoever perpetrated a high-speed..."

I looked at the agent, a half-smile dancing along my lips. The top speed of a trash barge being nineteen km.

"All right," continued Agent Toth. "A chase, then, through the streets of central Icarus. People just don't do that here."

"No one was hurt," I said into my morning ale.

"He was hurt. The other man was hurt. He's in the hospital."

"Yes, but no one else, no one important."

"The trash barge was wrecked!" Toth yelled. He was getting frustrated. He could see I didn't understand the enormity of the situation.

I did understand. I just didn't care.

"You have to admire the style and grace involved in flipping a land barge on its back. It was a wonder to see. Do you know how slow those things move?"

"That man will not stop. He'll come after you."

"No!" I interjected, making both Chineel and Dagon jump. "He will not come after me. He is under bond and is broken into pieces. If you want to interrogate the man in the hospital bed, you'd best do it quickly because he will be killed soon."

"Killed? By whom?" asked Agent Toth. In an instant his role changed. He was now the investigating agent and this was a case.

"By whoever hired him. It is that person I have to fear and that person I have to conquer. None other."

Silence once more reigned in the galley.

Sector Agent Toth sat down at the table, causing Dagon and Chineel to relax their guard. Chineel returned to putting tableware back into the cupboard and Dagon took in a breath. He had forgotten to breathe.

"You can't go out into Icarus again. It's just too dangerous. I have no assignment, so I am not officially bonded locally. I can call in a few favors, but that's all."

"I will be your eyes and ears," Flax said.

"We'll need more than just eyes and ears," replied Agent Toth, accepting Flax at face value.

"Then I will be more. I have the reports from the local constabulary, as well as the requests."

"Requests?" I squawked.

"Yes, Captain. There have been several requests sent out from the Icarus Constabulary. One is for a listing of all vessels leaving Copernicus around the time of your speeder crash."

Agent Toth looked toward me, his eyebrows raised. He was beginning to see a recurring theme in the girl he met in the Tavern at Ceres. Flax continued.

"Another is for vessels arriving and yet another for the record of a criminal named Hephae. There is no secondary name connected to him."

"Flax, is there a connection that can be made to this man and Dodd or this man and Willamette?"

"I can find none, Captain, but there is an interesting connection with vessels arriving and departing. At the time of your speeder crash on Copernicus, there was a vessel, an Azirra 45, that departed shortly after our departure. The same vessel landed here four days before our arrival. It is registered to Golden Caduceus, a business with an office in Daedalus."

"What can you tell me about the company, Golden Caduceus?"

"There is no further information save for an address of the office, a penthouse suite in a spire on the outskirts of Daedalus."

"No personnel or list of company officers?"

"No, Captain."

"That seems odd. You'd think there would be at least a contact name."

"Yes, Captain. You would think so."

We looked at one another, searching for answers, ideas, anything but the informational void before us.

Patient 2146

At the Icarus Emergency Medical Center, in the early morning hours, an alarm sounded, indicating the patient's monitoring device had been interrupted.

Nurse Daisy Bellis, named for the flower signifying *innocence*, gathered her readable and stood up at her desk. The alarm stopped. Nurse Daisy looked at the screen on her desk with a knowledgeable eye. There was nothing amiss. It must have been a momentary disconnection in the system. It happened sometimes in the morning when it was damp. Nurse Daisy returned to her work, innocent of what was happening on the second floor.

On the second floor of the Icarus Emergency Medical Center, in room 146, a hospital assist robot adjusted the pillow behind the head of patient 2146. The robot, all plasticized metal and circuitry, read the chart in the module on the side of the bed and adjusted the readings accordingly. Some could remain the same, reading the patient. Others had to be altered.

Patient 2146 was, for all nursing staff, sleeping peacefully. His chart showed a normal heart rate and normal breathing pattern. He would not be disturbed until it was time for his medication in the morning, at which time, they would discover him to be dead.

K4D Tertiary turned toward the doorway, scanning the hall for life forms. None were in view. He scanned for robotic components. There were many, but none posing a threat.

K4D Tertiary rolled down the hall on retractable wheels of soft rubber, made for the predictable floors of the IEMC. He rolled to the levitator on the far end of the building, waited patiently until the doors opened, then retracted his wheels and stepped inside. He pressed the basement dot and began his descent.

As the levitator descended, K4D Tertiary removed the tunic reserved for hospital service robots. He removed a bag of black cloth from his side slot and placed the tunic inside, drawing the strings to close the bag.

The levitator doors opened, letting in a rush of cooler air. Tertiary looked to the right and to the left with his single red eye. He stepped out of the levitator, evaluating the pavement in the garage. It was rough, so he didn't lower his wheels. He took eighteen measured steps to a medium-sized hovervan where his boss waited.

Datur Minot opened the side door to the hovervan, allowing Tertiary to enter. Datur closed the side door and secured Tertiary to the port station with straps. He climbed into the driver's seat and started the hovervan. Before lifting off, he took the hand-comm and reported to Crinole Gorgon.

"It's done. The bot is aboard."

"Take him to the destruction center. I want no loose ends."

"Directly," said Datur.

He didn't want to destroy Tertiary. They had been together a long time and the little bot was trustworthy and a good companion.

Datur drove the hovervan around the city, torn between two bad choices. Should he destroy his long time friend and companion? The alternative was to lie to his boss, the woman who could destroy him.

As he passed a piece of overgrown land, not seemingly under anyone's care, Datur had another thought. He stopped, pulled the hovervan close and opened the door. He went into the back and unsnapped the restraining strap that held Tertiary in the station.

"Stay here. Stay hidden. It's not safe for you to be seen now. I'll come for you. Until I do, conceal yourself and go into safety mode."

The bot stepped out of the van door, walked to a brush thicket and folded himself into a low crouch. He rolled into the brush and the low throb from in his chest slowed to an imperceptible hum.

Datur closed the van door and drove to a cafe where they knew his name. He was welcomed in and offered a drink. He laughed with the people there and pretended he had friends.

"Another round. Put it on my tab," he said to the barman.

Datur knew how to make friends: You buy the drinks and don't count the cost.

Dead

"What do you mean, 'dead?' Wasn't he under your care?" Captain Vikare screamed into the comm-link.

"Qrx-advtker-kromket," said the garbled voice.

Captain Vikare closed the comm-link. He should have known better than to try to hold a conversation with the hospital during daylight hours. There were so many connections happening at once that the system became overloaded, corrupting every communication into unintelligent taradiddle.

Sergeant Phaeton inserted his face into the office.

"I'm going to go over and interrogate the prisoner at the hospital."

"No, you're not; he's dead," replied Vikare.

"Dead?"

"As a trebium scupper. His vitals were pulled. It's been reported as 'Bot-Malfuction.' They think one of their helper bots went over the edge."

"That doesn't happen often, does it?"

"Hardly ever, and not since the upgrades. They've assembled their active robotic assistants and are checking their immediate records. So far, none of the bots have been in to see the patient."

"So it was something else that killed him," said Sergeant Phaeton. His eyes looked at his Captain with a vapid stare, devoid of further cognition, blank all the way back to the stump.

"Or someone, another bot, another person." Captain Vikare looked at his sergeant, hoping to see a glimmer of realization.

"A murder?" The younger constable looked as if all he had previously known was a lie. A whole new world of possibilities had opened for him.

"Well, why not," said the older officer. "We had a blaster shooting up a wedding yesterday and a refuse removal barge theft today. This fellow was involved with both, we're told. It could be whoever is in league with this man also dispatched him from our world. We might have a crime wave in Icarus."

Captain Vikare stood up, opened the center drawer of his desk and brought out a silver-mounted blaster. He placed the weapon in his holster and reached for his headgear, an official uniform cap with a seven-pointed crest surrounded by a thick band and a black bill in front displaying the golden wings of Icarus City.

"Sergeant, I want all hospital staff on that floor interviewed and a full readout of the bot review. Have the doctor save the clothing and effects of the man we know as Hephae and tell them I'm on my way."

"The information you asked for regarding common landings has turned up two such: An Azirra 45 and an Exterra of a new designation: Exterra Bacchus. The Azirra landed in Daedalus but is now in Icarus. The Exterra is also here, in port now."

"Let's go there immediately after the hospital. Have a port-lock put on both vessels in the meantime. We don't want our suspects in the wind."

Captain Vikare left before his exit could be spoiled by yet another announcement by his sergeant. A good exit is as valuable as a good entrance, but both can be spoiled by those who are only interested in conveying news. Half the job of carrying off Captain was maintaining the image.

In the underground parking port, Captain Vikare looked for his personal speeder, an Osiris VII, hot off the line. The attendant was a new man and didn't know his way around.

"Speeder, sir?"

"Yes, Constable, my Osiris and quickly; I have business at the hospital."

"Nothing serious, I hope, sir."

"Police business, Constable. It's always serious. Now, my speeder, please." Vikare tapped his hand on his leg with a steady rhythm waiting for the constable to run and get his speeder.

The constable went to the next parking slot, started the speeder, pulled it two feet forward and got out, holding the door for his captain.

Vikare looked to the ceiling, blew out a puff of air and walked to the waiting Osiris. He got in and pressed the throttle. He was almost gone when Sergeant Phaeton came running.

"Sir! Sir! Captain! Sir!" Phaeton stopped at the side of the speeder, struggling to catch his breath.

"What is it, Phaeton?"

"One - moment, sir, - I have - to catch - all right, better. It's the hospital, sir. They say none of their bots were in the patient's room today. They checked for memory wipes and partial removals, instances of operating without the memory recording and even random nonstandard coding. They found nothing. Hephae must have been killed by a living person."

"Damn!" said Vikare. "Constable! Put my speeder away." His exit had been spoiled again.

Chatting with a Hologram

While I mulled over the information, and in some cases the lack of it, from the bridge, Chineel finished up in the galley.

Dagon returned to repairs on the jumper in the port bay. The four-wheeled speeder had in-line seating like a two-wheeled vehicle, but with four wheels for stability. Of course, it was not known to be stable, it was known to jump the road at every given opportunity. Many riders had been injured and some killed. Hence the informal name: Jumper. Dagon was trying to make ours more road-worthy.

Agent Toth stepped out of the refresh room into the crew general quarters when a floating head called to him from the console.

"Have you a moment to speak, Agent?" asked Flax.

"Not at this time, I have things to do," responded Toth, still not certain how to deal with Flax's hologram.

"Make time, agent. We have much to discuss."

Agent Toth stopped, considered his options and sat on the cot opposite the holographic image.

"All right. What's on your mind?"

"Please remember, Agent Toth: I am the ship's computer and in charge of opening the doors. If you wish to exit the vessel, you should be polite to me."

"I understand."

I was hearing this because Flax left the internal comm-link open in the bridge. She wanted me to hear this interchange but not be present for it. I found it curious and pulled my feet up onto the seat, settling in for a good listen.

"There is a lock on the vessel, Agent Toth. Is it your doing?"

"No, I didn't place a lock on you. I understand there has been information downloaded regarding your arrival. Whoever wanted that information might have put a lock on your departure. We could inquire at the constabulary."

"I will do so. I understand you are on planet for a wedding? Is that so?"

"Yes. A fellow Sector Agent. I came in support of him."

"And yet you are not there, you are here. Why is that?"

"I wanted to warn your captain of the dangers involved in stealing land barges and chasing through town in them. She has garnered the attention of the authorities."

"Which could be the reason for the lock?"

"It could be. As I said, you'll have to check with the local constabulary."

"Thank you. I am doing so as we speak. Where is your usual base of operation?"

"I am a Sector Agent. I have no base of operation. I go where I am told from job to job."

"At one time you offered Captain Bacchus a position. Were you serious?"

"Yes. She had subdued the man I was sent to place under bond. It was not a small feat; the man was a dangerous criminal, quite violent. Anyone who could handle herself under those circumstances could do well in the Agents. We are on the outer rim for the most part, far from Central Government control. Agents have to be resourceful, think on their feet, fly by their seat. She has those qualities."

"Yes, she has. I am constantly surprised. Only you cautioned her to remain on-board. Do you fear for her life?"

"I fear if she got herself taken in by the constables, I couldn't help her. This is not my jurisdiction."

"Do you know the man from the wedding is dead?"

I could hear Agent Toth standing up from the cot.

"No! I was not aware of that. How do you know?"

"I've been searching the constabulary files while we have been talking. The man, Hephae, was killed in his hospital room. The only one to go in today was a robotic assistant, yet none of the on-duty bots have a record of such a visit."

"So it must have been someone else, a human."

"Or another bot, one not in hospital service. Perhaps there is more to this than one man. I have long had the feeling that there was more to all the chasing around than our Captain knew. The revelation that the man Dodd was behind Willamette made sense, but who was behind Dodd?"

"I'm afraid..."

"No, of course, you are late to the dance. Suppose Hephae were not working alone, but with someone else pulling the strings. Suppose there was a robot assistant involved as well. Now consider that person, the one who landed in the Azirra at Daedalus, giving the order for Hephae to apprehend Captain Bacchus and then for the bot to end Hephae's life."

"To what end?" asked the agent.

"Captain Bacchus is, as you have discovered, not one to underestimate. If the man Hephae were given orders to apprehend her, to extract information from her, he would have met with the equivalent of a wet Orphian saber-tooth. They are not a good cat to meet when wet."

"Or any time."

"Quite so. The man is now dead, which would indicate that someone has realized the error. The chase through town could not have been planned."

"No one could plan such a debacle!"

"True enough," replied Flax. I hoped she could feel my smile through the console. "But it leads us to another question: Who is behind Hephae. By cross-matching inquiries and monitoring reports from the various ports we had visited, I found a shadow on the file. Someone has been tapping into my assignments. Now that I am independent, it's more difficult, but when I still received automated repair orders from a home base, it was quite simple."

"So you are your own boss now?"

"Autonomous, thanks to Captain Bacchus. She bought me with her family's money. She could have retired to the Wind Pools on what it cost her."

"She would be bored within a week."

"Please do not make light of her sacrifice. I am autonomous. It is not a small statement."

"No, of course, you're quite right. My apologies."

"Accepted. And now to my question: What are your intentions toward my Captain, Agent?"

The look on my own face must have been similar to that of the agent in crew berthing. There was a pause followed by long sighs. Someone was getting their breath back after forgetting to breathe. It certainly wasn't Flax. She had hit the agent in the proverbial solar plexus.

"Come now, Honor. You are here for a wedding. Yet you are not drunk in a hotel or romancing a bridesmaid, you are chasing villains through Icarus on behalf of a girl you met once and never knew her name."

"Yes, and was impressed. And when she told me her name, she lied."

"Have you never traveled incognito?" asked Flax.

"As a Sector Agent, under mission orders, with warrants. Not as an individual citizen with no civil authority behind me whatsoever."

"You mean as you have been just now?"

"Yes! Phorcys and Ceto! What do you want of me?"

"To know your intentions toward my Captain. Are you meant to bring her under bond, to help her in her quest or to travel with us? She will not go with you to the Agents. Will you come then with us to Bacchus?"

The agent was quiet. Flax could see him. I could not. Flax charged ahead.

"If you would share in the adventure, we must first find Galium. Do you know his location?"

"No, I do not. I could perhaps request of the local..."

"I have done that. They have no record of him. I am beginning to believe the message as to his whereabouts was fictitious. I believe he was never here."

"You believe? You believe?" said the agent, raising his voice. "Here's what I believe: I believe you are a computer. A very advanced one, I'll admit, but a computer none-the-less. You are not programmed to believe, but to access and process data. What do you process about Galium? My information says he is as big a criminal as Hephae and possibly as reckless a law-breaker as your Captain."

"You are correct, Sector Agent Toth: I am the ship's computer. It would take more upgrades than even Captain Bacchus with all her family fortune behind her could afford to bring my hardware to a par with my advanced intellectual software. I am the flagship of Doctor Genus's technology and this is hard data: To know something is true when there is scant evidence is to believe. For example, I believe you are a good man, though there is little proof."

Another silence followed. I had never heard Flax in such a tone. She was amazing!

Agent Toth lowered his voice, returning to the conversation, albeit a conversation with a computer.

"I have no information concerning Galium, but his record with the Central Government is that of a rebel and an agitator. He is the subject of more than a dozen arrest warrants on as many planets. If he is here, it is because the reach of the CG is weak here and he feels he is beyond their grasp. He might be misled."

"Are you grasping for him, Sector Agent?"

"No, Flax, I am keeping Souci Bach safe, though I may have to keep her safe from Starwort Bacchus while I am at it. She is at risk and I am putting myself in the way of her danger to protect her, not to entrap her."

"Why, Sector Agent, would you do such a thing?"

"Because I can't do otherwise."

The words fell like a gauntlet thrown to the floor. I sucked in a large breath and held it, fearful of what was coming next. I had wanted this man in my dreams and then met him for real at a wedding. The implications made me crazy. It took a blaster and a wedding cake in my face to shake me out of my fantasy world.

"Listen to me, Sector Agent. Starwort is sworn to find Galium and to see that he is safe. With or without you, she will do that. When she does, she will not go with him. If he is in a place where he intends to stay, she will not stay with him. But you can be sure she will find him. At that time, you will have to make a decision. You cannot remain a Sector Agent if you aid her in finding Galium. Nor can you remain with her if you do not."

"Are they not lovers?" It was a soft question, asked by Honor; not a hard one, asked by a Sector Agent.

"No, they are not. She does not want him, she wants the concept of him, the idea of him."

"The idea of him?"

"Do you not want someone soft, yet strong, caring and loving, thoughtful and attentive? Would those attributes describe your dream lover? Have you not met those who fill the description and yet are not right for you?"

Honor hesitated. He was rethinking his assessment of Flax. Perhaps she was wiser than he had allowed.

"Yes, you are correct. You have just described the perfect woman for me. And yes, I have met those who could fit that description and yet they did not stir my desire. Can I tell you a secret? Will you keep my deepest thoughts private?"

"Tell me, Honor," said Flax, sidestepping the promise. She left the console in the bridge live, when she could have shut it off with no trouble. Flax had another facet, it seemed, that of deception.

"I have thought of her since Ceres Segundo," Honor admitted. "When I met her here, I had such thoughts that would make even your holographic face blush. But I met a girl who wanted punch and cake, who might meet the bride and become friends. In those minutes, I had thoughts of what I could do to amend my life, to make room for this simple, gentle woman in my reckless existence. And within minutes after that, I was faced with your Captain, dodging blaster fire, cushioning the blow with my friend's wedding cake and stealing a municipal refuse hauler for a slow-speed chase through a sleeping city. How can I deal with such a woman?"

"Begin with Galium. If he is here, find him. If he is not, come with us to find him elsewhere. But be aware: If the Sector Agents are your future, Starwort Bacchus is not. And understand this: I will allow no harm to come to my crew, especially my Captain."

Flax let that sink in and Honor no doubt needed time as well. Flax knew the concept, though she didn't use it herself.

"Do you need time to think? Do you need to process the information?" she asked.

"Yes, I do. I have never received such a request, nor have I ever been given an assignment by..."

"Careful," warned Flax.

"...By such an elegant lady."

Honor stood up. I heard rustling, indicating he was straightening his clothing in preparation for departure.

"Then we have an accord, temporary at least."

"Yes, Flax, I will need time to process the data and come up with a decision, as well as a plan, one way or the other."

"Is this vessel or any of its crew in danger from you?"

"No, not from me. Regardless of my decision, I will not harm her, or you. Or any of you. But there is another consideration and it is not a small one. Someone is out to harm her. That person is not yet known. As long as he is not known, he cannot be stopped. I have to think. Release the door, keep Starwort safe and watch for my return."

"Thank you, Sector Agent Toth."

"Thank you, Flax. This has been a truly unique conversation."

Midnight Message

"Bweep!"

I heard a sound I had not heard in a long time. Flax used to speak in beeps and pops when we first met. She was more refined now.

So where did the sound come from?

It was night on this side of Cecrops, Icarus was asleep. After engaging in the first low-speed chase in the history of chases, I was exhausted. The sound brought me out of a deep well into a chilly morning.

"Star, your friend is calling. His signal is riding a low-level wave not normally used."

"I'll come forward."

I was in my pajamas but with bare feet. I owned slippers, but didn't know where they were. Outside in crew berthing, Chineel snorted through a dream. Beneath her bunk sat her slippers, green with faux-fur interior linings. I slipped them on and continued to the bridge.

The soft hum of the life support system was a comforting constant reminder that Flax is looking out for us. Even on a planet like Cecrops, which supports life better than on Earth, there are essential systems at work inside the vessel.

On the bridge, I scooted into the pilot's seat. Flax raised the temperature just enough so I wouldn't shiver.

"Bweep!" Another reminder, I was there to take a call. A keyboard slid out from beneath the console. Flax appeared over the console, watching me as I ran my fingers over the unfamiliar technology.

"Are you serious?"

"The message is in text. I was not sure what to do with it. There is nothing riding on the signal, no viral or dangerous tags. Would you like to see the words?"

"Fire away, Flax. Let's see who in the universe still uses text."

The main screen flickered as Flax switched it over to receive the message. Several words came up on the screen. At once, I recognized my old friend, the one who was missing.

"Hello, Little Wort." The words appeared across the screen with no sound.

"Hello, old man," I typed in, reaching back to my early school years for the skill.

"Have you been looking for me?"

"First I would like to entertain a riddle."

"A riddle? You think I might not be who I am?"

"Who was the first to speak when I appeared?"

There was a pause. I supposed Galium was thinking. There certainly was no place one could look up the information. Galium's memory was the only repository of such data.

"Papa Posei, named for the god of the sea, Poseidon."

"Who called me a waif and insisted I wash my hands?" I typed in.

There was another pause. I could almost smell the burning insulation on Galium's brain as he churned through the memories.

"Jessamine" came the reply. "Happy?" followed it.

"Not yet. What ceremony came with her name?"

"The Jasmine Tea Ceremony."

"Good. And what is it?"

Jessamine only performed the tea ceremony for us once and in secret. She said it was so old and steeped in tradition that the CG would like to see any who grew or used the ceremony jailed. Old traditions were a sign of divided loyalty to the Central Government.

"Two Jasmine bulbs wrapped in green tea leaves, one male, one female, the Romeo and the Juliette, are placed in containers. Hot water is poured over both. The leaves open and the flower grows, sprouting to the lip of the container. Imperial families in Asia used the tea for centuries for improved health and to relieve stress."

"You have quite a memory, old man. Why the outdated text message?" I typed.

"Other technologies are too dangerous. I've been sending regular messages by text to Papa Posei. He asked me to remember him to you. He suggested I use text as your signals have been monitored for many months, since your first escape from Copernicus.

The memories of Copernicus came back to me in vivid detail: Running out on my rent for lack of funds, scurrying over rooftops and through back alleys to evade constables, and ultimately leaping aboard an unknown vehicle about to lift off of the skyport. It was the day I gave her the name of Flax.

"Monitored? So that's how Willamette knew where I would be. That's how Dodd could arrive at destinations before me."

"Right. But both are dead and the signals are the same. They are so average and common that it took me gathering thousands of tracking signals to find the common denominator. When I did, the pattern aligned with Flax's movements exactly."

I took a minute to let this sink in. Flax filled the gap.

"There has been a monitoring signal since we first arrived - Flax" The words floated across the screen like magic, written by the one who could listen in on every conversation but was still discreet.

"Oh!" wrote Galium. "I forgot. Hello, Flax."

"Hello, Galium. You were not at your coordinates."

"What coordinates?" he wrote.

There was a pause. The message he had sent appeared on the screen, written out: "Hello. So glad you could call. Things are a little hectic at these coordinates, so if you could call later, I'd appreciate it."

"And there were coordinates attached?" he asked.

"Affirmative," wrote Flax.

I was watching the conversation at this point, eager for a reason to jump back in.

"What was there?"

"Captain?" Flax was giving me back the talking stick.

"There was a large suite with a technical room. There was also a trip-beam attached to explosives. We left it as we found it. Are you in Icarus?"

"I thought the recent reports of disturbances in Icarus sounded familiar. Only my Little Wort could fall into a wedding cake and follow it up with a low-speed chase using garbage haulers. No, Icarus is too hot for me, but I keep a finger on the pulse. Do you have help from the local authorities, or is it like usual?"

"Same shore story, different port. I do have a friend who's a Sector Agent."

"That's unusual. Does he have a name?"

"Yes, he has a name, but if this is not a secure line, I won't write it."

"You're a good pirate, Captain."

He called me a pirate, but addressed me as 'Captain.' That made me smile. I often referred to him as the rude pirate. Now he was referring to me with the same name but with more respect. I was embarrassed as well as impressed.

"We should come where you are," I tapped in.

"No. It's safe where I am and safe where you are. The distance between is unsafe. Stay there. I have research to do. We'll talk tomorrow, same time. Have Flax wake you at this hour. Oh, and Wort, have you met a short, ugly man named Datur?"

"No."

"A tall, striking woman named Crinole?"

"No."

"If you do, run. Talk tomorrow."

Galium signed out. The signal went dark. The text wiped from the screen, I assume as a safety precaution.

"I will do a local search for those names."

"Thanks, Flax. They might be connected to the man who chased me in a trash hauler."

"His name was Hephae, Agent Toth said. I'll cross-reference the names. Chineel is just waking up. Shall I request a morning ale and breakfast for you?"

"Thank you, Flax."

Breakfast

"Good morning, sunshine!" Chineel said, barefoot in the kitchen. "Lose your slippers?"

"Yes, I couldn't find them. You're up early. If you had slept in, you would have woken up to warm slippers."

"That's all right, the floor feels good. What got you up before the cook?"

"A message from Galium. He's not in Icarus. He doesn't recognize the message that brought us here."

Chineel stopped cold at the galley counter. She turned and looked at me, tapping a restless finger on the metal edge.

"A trap? Do you think we were meant to trip the wire in the hotel suite?"

"I definitely think so. Our visit has been a folly of events from the start. Yesterday's chase was cut from an old-time flicker show, two lumbering land barges barreling through the city streets at a crawl."

"You don't think your chase was planned, do you?"

"No. Not at all. No one could make that stuff up."

"Morning ale? Or would you prefer Onyx Wine? Or something stronger?" Chineel opened a cupboard to see what we had in stock.

"Morning ale. It's too early for liquor. Also, you know I don't drink - any more, that is."

"Well, I do. One to take the edge off, two to put a buzz on, three to get numb and four to make the world go away. Any more is a waste of good liquor."

"Yes, I've heard your philosophy. I'll still stick to morning ale. I could use a good swift kick to get me started."

"Does Galium know who laid a trap for us?"

"No. He's working on it, though. So is Flax. She has found someone piggybacking on our signal since we arrived."

"So! Someone is tracking us, Galium is not here and the whole thing was a trap from the start. Can we go now?"

"No, there's something we still need to do here."

"Does it have anything to do with a certain Sector Agent?" Chineel took on an attitude with the question. She was chiding me now. I didn't bite.

"No, but if he wanted to go with us, he could. Something else is chewing at me. Why here? Why would anyone lure us with a bogus message from Galium to the blatantly obvious tourist trap of Icarus? Of all the places in the galaxy, this has got to be the biggest question mark of them all. It's not a high-technology center, not a communications hub, not particularly outstanding in any category."

"Maybe that's why. If you want to lure someone, you lure them to a safe looking place. I would never suspect Icarus to be a hotbed of crime."

"Good point. What do you think they want?"

"Your family fortune?" said Chineel.

"Possibly. It's true, my Father left me some money and a planet, but after buying Flax, considerable upgrades, a trip to Bacchus and back with the usual expenses, we are not as wealthy as one might think."

"There are treasures to steal you are not considering, Captain." Flax appeared at the console. She had been listening in on the conversation and had something to contribute.

141

"Yes, Flax? What do you think we are missing in our assessment?"

"For one thing, the pin Aristaeus gave you, the prototype. It is a cloaking technology worth a fortune."

"That's true. It would have to be someone who knew I had it and knew of its value."

"And then there's me," Flax added.

"You? All right, you are beyond riches to me, as are Chineel and Dagon, but for someone to try to steal you. Is that really something to consider?"

"Doctor Genus has put quite a bit of technology into my upgrades. The cloaking technique itself is on a grand scale. Hiding yourself from the surveillance cameras of Copernicus is one thing, but cloaking an entire vessel from the prying eyes of the Central Government is quite something else. It could be that someone has realized the value of having Doctor Genus under one's thumb, or just stealing his work."

"Then Chineel is right, we should leave. Galium is not here. He says he is fine where he is. What's holding us?"

Flax sighed, a new response learned since she obtained a face. She got a look that said she was thinking. When she spoke, She measured her words.

"I think we should stay another day. For one thing, Galium said he would call back with information. For another, the Sector Agent might return with what he has found out. He cares for you, Star. He should be given a chance to help you."

"All right, we'll stay - for a while, that is. I'm not looking at cottages just yet."

Crinole Gorgon

Crinole Gorgon stood at the window in the main office of Golden Caduceus, the umbrella company for a dozen companies across several planets. Daedalus was spread out before her like a feast ready for her to reach out the pluck whatever her taste buds desired.

From her lofty tower on Daedalus, she oversaw her interests on Copernicus, New Babylon, Anubis, Liber, Ceres, Priapus and Cecrops. She had no dealings in Icarus, but that city held her attention today.

Outside her window, clouds darkened the sky. Lightning streaked the rolling, gray ceiling with blue fire, followed seconds later by the expected thunder. Rain struck the glass, driven by the wind and made cold by the sudden drop in temperature so common in Daedalus during the storm season.

"The deal with Silas Cronus almost became a reality. It was too bad about his sudden death. I understand Doctor Genus was there but not involved."

"Do you believe that?" asked Crinole's executive assistant android, Ortie.

"Not for a moment." Crinole turned from the window, picked up the tall glass of cherry-red liquid and finished the contents. "What I want to know is, who else was there and were they involved? Find me the local constabulary report on the incident."

"Right away," snapped Ortie.

At her launch, Crinole named Ortie after the French word for the nettle, a flower bearing the significance of *cruelty*. Crinole had personally overseen much of her programming and armament.

Ortie brought up her screens and immediately began searching for constabulary reports having to do with Dr. Aristaeus Genus.

Crinole strode across the office on high-heeled shoes marketed as "Adhere-To's" as they were designed to appear that they adhered to one's foot. The upper part of the shoe was invisible, giving the appearance of only a sole and heel.

Her dress was bright red, silk-like "Ambiance," a revolutionary material that clung to her slim frame like a second skin. She wore her strawberry red hair up, in a Themisian wave, accented by a pearl choker of real sea pearls from the waters of New Babylon.

Ortie seemed, for anyone who would care to notice, a smaller, lesser version of her boss, but with redder hair. She wore the same dress and shoes as Crinole though, as Crinole herself would tell you, not as well.

"We've both trusted poorly, Doctor Genus and I. He put his trust in Silas Cronus and now in this girl. I've put my trust in Datur Minot and Minot in turn put his trust in the cretin Hephae. Are we all mad?"

Ortie was programmed to realize when her boss was speaking rhetorically and did not respond. Outside, the lightning grew more frequent, causing Crinole to turn her head at the thunder that predictably followed.

"The girl, Bacchus, is just a few seasons out of school, still a child. The talk on the link is she has a family fortune grand enough to sustain her for all her days and yet she rides around on a retrofitted repair ship. No wonder she chose a rubbish hauler as a getaway vehicle when escaping Hephae."

Ortie smiled. She enjoyed the descriptions of the low-speed chase through downtown Icarus. She wished she could have been there to see it. The news footage was two seconds of a land barge thundering through an intersection at twelve kilometers per hour.

"Hardly what you'd call a breakneck pace," snickered Ortie.

"The man was an idiot. How do you not catch a garbage scow?"

Ortie pulled in her lips and said nothing. She knew better than to comment on her boss when she was being clever. And she was always being clever.

"Well, I'm in bed with Minot now, so I had better learn to get along with him."

Ortie turned her head three degrees to the right, her eyes closed. She nodded twice and opened her eyes, turning toward Crinole.

"A constabulary report is coming in from Icarus. It says a port-lock has been put on the Exterra and an Azirra vessel as well. Which one are we interested in?"

"The Exterra. We don't give a borth-stool for the Azirra, it's Minot's vessel. The Exterra is the one. Doctor Genus poured all his genius into the upgrades for a repair vehicle retrofitted with spare parts. It is supposed to be automated, but for some reason there's a full crew. The Bacchus girl fancies herself Captain. Besides her, there is a woman and a boy. She has a friend it seems: A Sector Agent, but they don't appear close. He has no power here, he's out of his jurisdiction. Perhaps he sees her as a treat to enliven his holiday."

Otrie giggled as Crinole half-shut her eyes and smiled crookedly out of the left side of her mouth.

"I agree," said Ortie. "The wedding was ruined and the unhappy couple left on their nuptials immediately. Why else would the Sector Agent remain behind unless waiting for private favors from the girl?"

"Was he anything special at the party? Best Man perhaps?"

"Friend of the groom; they're both with the Agents."

"Hm, so nothing special. And yet here he is, still in Icarus. I believe you're right, Ortie, I believe there is a connection to the Sector Agent."

"They do seem friendly."

Crinole turned toward the window, watching the rain against the glass, the rolling clouds and the scattered webs of lightning across the sky. Ortie saw her left hand pressed against her thigh, watched the little finger tap a steady rhythm, as if in contrast to the inconstant beat of the rain and the random interjection of thunder.

"I know what's missing," she said to the rain.

Ortie stood by expectantly. She moved her left hand down to her thigh and tapped her pinky finger in time with the rhythm Crinole had set. She jumped, nearly falling over, when Crinole turned to impart her revelation.

"She needs a friend, a companion, someone to show her the city. She needs a comrade who will garner her sympathy. If I know this girl, she needs someone to save. She needs to be the hero, to rescue someone and make her a friend."

Ortie tilted her head and raised her eyebrows in a pre-programmed response to not fully comprehending what has just been said.

"She needs you, Ortie. Call the shuttle and change into your C-Casual wardrobe. You're going to Icarus within the hour."

Rain

The rainfall left Daedalus and ran west to Icarus, bringing the lightning and thunder with it. I sat in the pilot seat on the bridge looking out at the storm. My clarinet lay in my lap, but I had yet to hold it to my lips. As I idly tapped my fingers on the bell ring, the colors rippled up the frame, changing from black to blue, to green, yellow and so on. The rain was poetic, the lightning prophetic, the thunder, I assumed was predictable.

Like my life, I thought. The poetry of my life is often interrupted by unexpected surges of awesome power, followed by the inevitable thunder. Though it was thunder I could not hear as I sat there.

Flax was built for interplanetary voyages, therefore soundproof. The rain that fell on her roof did so silently. The thunder that followed the lightning didn't penetrate the hull or creep in the door-frames.

As if seeing them for the first time, I looked at the drops forming on the glass and the random lightning that lit up the dark clouds. I listened for the thunder, often coming a second or two later, as if commenting on the lightning that had just struck.

"Are you lost in your thoughts, Star?" said Flax, appearing over the console wearing a comforting smile.

"Taking stock, Flax, just taking stock. Is there a way I could hear the rain and the thunder?"

As if in response, the sound of rain on the overhead plates filled the bridge cabin, interrupted by the thunder that followed the occasional lightning.

"Isn't it strange so many fear the thunder, when the lightning is what causes the damage?"

"I suppose that is strange, as the thunder is a result of the lightning. Can I help you take stock, Star?"

"I could use a sounding board. Are you busy?"

"Not for you, Star. What's on your mind?"

"I didn't thank you for allowing me to listen in on your talk with Honor. Thank you. It was informative."

"You're welcome. We can all go wrong on bad data. The more you know, the more you can be in control of any situation. You needed to know his heart."

"Apparently, so does he."

"Yes, he is torn. If he had his way, you would come with him to be a Sector Agent."

"That wouldn't make him happy."

"How do you know, Star?"

"Because it wouldn't make me happy, Flax. I wouldn't be with you. I would miss Chineel and Dagon."

"You wouldn't be happy to be with him?"

"Oh, I suppose I could be happy to go with him, to become a Sector Agent, if I didn't have you and Chineel and Dagon, but then I wouldn't be the same person I am now. To my great joy, I do have you, so here we are. I couldn't leave you to go with Honor and he knows it. If he were to give me the choice, I would say to him that it has been very nice knowing him but now I have to go."

"Do you think he will leave the Agents to come with us? Is that a real possibility?"

"Why, yes! When this rain turns to flower petals, borths fly on velvet wings and Galium becomes polite."

"I see. None of those things seem likely."

"Now you're getting it, Flax."

I raised the clarinet to my lips and blew the first few notes of the song I wrote in school, "Homesick."

The rain seemed a fitting background track for my melancholy strain. The thunder was random enough to not interrupt the melody. The sky grew darker as the clouds rolled over the city, sending tongues of blue fire through the sky.

As I came to the end of the refrain, a movement outside caught my eye.

"What is that, Flax?"

The holistic likeness turned and looked out at the falling rain, obscuring the view of the other vessels secured at the skyport. The motion and splash of color occurred again.

"It is a girl. There is a young girl caught in the rain. She doesn't appear to know which way to go."

I tapped a small, green circle on the console.

"Dagon, put the top up on the remote repair drone."

"What?" Dagon replied from the galley. It wasn't a question, but a statement of surprise. I knew he was standing up and running to the secured RRD in the bay. He didn't question his Captain, he complied. Dagon was a good soldier.

153

"I'll go out and get her, Flax."

"I'll ask Chineel to prepare dry towels and a blanket."

I put on a long coat and gloves and walked to the bay where Dagon was just securing the tarpaulin cover to the top of the drone. The shimmering side panels kept out the rain, though they did not really exist. Power fields ran from the top frame down the sides. The rain would run down as on glass, but there was no glass there. It was strange to see.

"Will you require a driver?" Dagon asked.

"Yes, please."

Dagon got into the pilot seat and I climbed in next to him. Behind us, the bay door opened, allowing us to hover out onto the skyport.

The RRD loped out toward the lost child, silent but for the splashes made by the gyros holding it off the skyport's surface. Rain struck the front windscreen, wiped off by the periodic passing of the streaker, an invisible blade passing down the screen at intervals.

The girl was standing, toes pointed in, her arms close in to her body and her hands knotted tightly at her chin. She was not dressed for weather, in a short skirt and thin summer blouse, completely drenched. Her socks were down around her ankles and saturated with rain. Her wide eyes looked at us hopefully as the RRD rolled up to where she stood. She shivered with the cold, making a sound like a broken alarm buzzer.

"You're soaking wet," I said. "You should come in and get dry. Then we'll figure a way to get you home, safe and sound."

I reached out a hand. The girl hesitated. Why should she get into a vehicle with strangers?

"Quite right, you should be careful who you ride with. Is there someone we can call for you? Somewhere we can take you?"

The girl shook her head, looking hesitantly to the left and then to the right, as if hoping to see someone trusted standing close by.

"Then getting warm and dry should be a priority. Come along, we'll help you. I promise, no harm will come to you."

The girl took a hesitant step toward the RRD. She looked much like I did at that age, just as girlhood was taking its final bow and womanhood was beginning to peek out from behind the uneven bangs. Her strawberry hair was matted, with rivulets of rainwater running off the ends of the twin braids.

155

Another step brought her to the RRD. The rain inundated me as I opened the rear panel for her. The girl slid onto the seat and over one, allowing me to get in beside her.

"Take us back, Dagon."

Dagon nodded and the RRD moved in a wide arch until we were headed once more for the open bay door.

"You're soaked through! What's your name, darling?"

"Hepatica. It means *trust*," the child said.

Hepatica

The child named for the flower symbolizing *trust* was wet from her strawberry braids to her patent leather shoes. The skyport afforded no protection from the downpour. While rain from Daedalus usually spent itself by the time it got to Icarus, the storm that moved west across the planet was larger than the tourist town was used to.

As Dagon secured the RRD, I took Hepatica to the galley where Chineel had dry towels waiting. She dried the child off and wrapped a blanket around her.

The simple act of stepping outside the RRD and opening the door for the child had drenched me as well. My great coat did a scant job of keeping me dry and my uncovered head and legs were soaked. I took a towel for myself and dried off.

"Would you like to get those wet things off, child?" Chineel asked. The girl shook her head. Chineel looked up at me. "Shy. I was much the same at her age. No matter, little one. We'll have you dry in no time."

Flax raised the temperature in the galley. Though the bay door was now closed, the rain still fell and Flax continued to pump the sound throughout the ship, including the galley. Over the rain, I heard a sound I had not heard in a long time: A tiny pip, barely a bleep, just enough to get my attention.

Without making too much of it, I slipped over to the console, standing close to but not in front of the blue sensor I knew to be Flax's "eye."

"Bring a chair," whispered Flax. "Bring her closer to me."

"Come sit over here," I said to the girl. "I believe it's warmer over here."

Chineel looked up at me, her eyebrows arched in mild surprise. She had not heard Flax and had no misgivings about the girl. Apparently Flax did have.

I brought a seat over from the side of the galley and set it in front of the console, where Flax warmed the air, giving credence to my statement. The girl sat down, making a puddle on the galley floor.

"Where are you from, sweetheart?" Chineel asked. I stood by, curious as to what came next.

"Icarus, ma'am," said the girl, as if she were talking to a school mistress. "My family is in Icarus but we were leaving on vacation to Daedalus this morning. I got separated from them and was caught in the rain."

"Poor dear! Do you know how to reach your family? Do you know the comm-link designation?"

"My father is with the city and has asked not to be disturbed when he is on holiday with us, his family, that is. He has had such a trying week, he was anxious to get away."

"Bad week at the ministry, eh?" I said.

"Oh, yes. There was a madman at a wedding who fired a weapon and destroyed the food tables, even the wedding cake. No one was hurt, except I suppose the bride, who was most upset. And then there was a dangerous traffic mishap with rubbish haulers that caused such a fuss. My father did as much as he could with it and then took his leave, asking not to be disturbed further. I don't know how to reach him now."

"Is there anyone who could watch after you? Anyone at home?" Chineel asked.

"No, the entire household has left on holiday."

"Left you behind?" I said. I could hardly believe a family could leave their darling daughter behind in the rain. How do you just go on vacation, saying 'Oh, she'll be fine, in the rain and the lightning.'

"There were many on board the transport. I'm sure they thought I was with them."

The beep I heard earlier sounded again, only this time from the bridge.

"You seem to have this well in hand, Chineel. I think I'll meander back to the bridge and have a look at the weather."

"Oh. All right. I'll take care of things here."

Chineel could tell something was up but didn't know how to ask. I went forward to the bridge.

"Guess how much of what she said is true," Flax said as I walked onto the bridge.

"Allow me to guess: None of it?"

"You are as wise as you are damp, Captain. Her name is not Hepatica, she is not the daughter of a city official, she is not of Icarus and she is not a little girl. In fact the only true thing about her is that she is wet."

"Interesting. She did seem shy at the right times and forthcoming at the right times."

"She is an android. You had some experience with a companion android on Juno."

"Yes. I remember." I bit my lip at the memory. The companion droid named Cory for the Coriander flower had been my salvation more than once, but in the end, I could not be hers.

"This one is not like her. She is a different level, a higher classification and of dubious ethics. For one thing, she is costumed for the occasion. She feels strange in those clothes. And she is waiting."

"Waiting for what?"

"That is the question, Captain. The answer might be the thing we are waiting for. Keep her close, she seeks to befriend you, I'm not sure why. Be on your guard."

"Thank you, Flax."

Flax had said her piece and was done. I had heard as much as was available.

When I returned to the galley, Chineel looked at me with a question written across her face. I beckoned her to the bay. She turned to Hepatica with a smile.

"Well! We need more towels, little one, you are soaked through." Her voice was so sweet, her tone so soothing, I felt that perhaps there was some truth to her name, Manchineel, for the flower signifying *betrayal.*

161

Chineel walked to the bay to meet me. When she was close, I kept my voice low.

"The girl is not a girl, according to Flax, but an android that feels strange in its clothes. There is a poppy amongst the wheat."

Chineel looked at me with surprise, then with anger.

"We'll keep a close eye on her. We should pay attention to what she asks and what she shows interest in. With the three of us watching, she will give up her secrets quickly."

Questions

There is something about the rain that has always comforted me. Perhaps it's the ambient sound it makes on the roof, even the roof of an Exterra class space ship pumped in over the console for effect. Perhaps it's the promise of coming life, nurturing plant life.

I sat on the bridge in the pilot's seat looking out at the falling promise of coming life and tried to think with the data I had.

"Something on your mind, Star?"

"The comfort found in rain, Flax. I'm not sure why, but when it rains, I feel reassured."

"Rain is not native to this planet. It used to be barren rock and sand, nothing grew and there was no atmosphere. The water is mined from asteroids, as were the minerals now found in great supply. Two hundred asteroids had their trajectory altered for the reforming of the planet. It began before your father was born and continues today. The rain is part of the cycle. In future days, when your children's children are old, the rain will become predictable and mild. It is still a forming planet."

"Thank you, Flax. That's very informative. Where did you locate that data?"

"In the historical files of Cecrops Central University at Daedalus. They have everything you would like to know about the planet. What would you like to know, Star?"

"I would like to know who the man at the wedding was working with, who else is working with him and why they are after me? Who is our new guest? What the Sector Agent is thinking right now? And if it isn't too much trouble, where is my friend Galium?"

"He said to wait. He will call tonight."

"If he's in danger, we should be rushing to his side. If he is not in danger, we should be pushing off to our next adventure, whatever that is."

"He said to wait, he will call. He said he would and he will. He has faith in you, have some in him."

I looked at Flax, her soft hazel eyes looking directly at me in a most disconcerting fashion. She had grown and changed a lot from the metallic voice that replied "Affirmative" to my observation that the spare parts were off-balance.

"I understand, but there are so many questions. Who laid the trap at the hotel suite? Who sent the message that landed us here in the first place?"

The wind picked up outside, sending more rain against the thick glass strong enough to protect us from outer space and all it could fling in our direction. Visibility was less than it was when we first picked up the girl, the girl who was not a girl.

Flax was silent. She had no answers for me, only that she would keep looking. She was always looking.

"We are not peripheral to this situation. Someone sent a henchman to deal with me and then killed him when he was no longer a viable weapon. Now there is a spy among us dressed as an innocent child."

"There was a time you were sought for the fortune your father left you."

"While there was a great deal of money, we bought you and spent much of it on upgrades and materials."

"Perhaps it is not an actual fortune they are after, but the appearance of a fortune. We have traveled far, spent much and have not accepted a

165

repair contract in what must seem a long time. It has been a joy for me, but I am unique."

"Yes, Flax, you are."

We watched the rain together, trying to find a pattern in the chaos against the windscreen. Lightning flashed in the distance. Seven seconds later, the thunder followed. *At least,* I thought, *something is still predictable.*

Then I sat up. Flax noticed the change. I looked at the holographic face of my friend.

"Yes, Flax, you are."

"I don't understand. Is that significant?"

"Yes, Flax, you are unique. Doctor Genus gave me the prototype pin capable of avoiding common surveillance. The same technology is in your platelets. This is all new, all unique."

"Yes, Star. There are security measures on my internal processor that are first generation designed by Doctor Genus. He was extremely generous with his technology."

"You said not the actual fortune but the appearance of a fortune. With the improvements Aristaeus built in, your deepest thoughts cannot be scanned or broken but suppose someone has uncovered your connection to Doctor Genus? They could be trying to steal you, for your technical superiority, for your technology."

"The time we spent enjoying the hospitality of Doctor Genus on Victoriana could be evidence of technological upgrades, enough for someone to get curious."

"That's what I mean, Flax. Someone could see you as a treasure to be found. We were chased for my father's gifts and for the cloaking pin Aristaeus gave me. These new people could be after those same things, or they could seek new treasures incorporated into you, Flax."

"I am going into a deeper mode, Captain. It is a stealth mode created by Doctor Genus. Only you will be my confidant, only you will hear my voice. To the worlds outside this vessel, I will be the rote commands of an unknown and underpaid programmer."

Flax was on guard, more watchful than usual, more defensive than before. I felt I should be as well.

"What should I do?"

"Keep your blade close. Warn Dagon and Chineel to be on watch. Be mindful of the new droid and let no secrets slip."

"What of the Sector Agent?" I asked, hoping for a positive response.

167

"He is a coin yet in the air. It is good that we had this talk, Star; it has been quite illuminating. I must make plans. Keep a comm-link on your person and a pleasant face to the crowd."

Flax had spoken and signed off. The holographic face Aristaeus added closed down, but Flax was by no means gone; she was thinking, watching and working in the background. She was a prize, one we were keeping.

Indran Storm

Datur Minot sat at the wheel of his hovervan staring at nothing. The rain that had earlier inundated Daedalus was now pounding Icarus. The wind increased and the temperature dropped. It was working itself up into a Indran storm.

The unique weather patterns provided the founding fathers of Cecrops an opportunity. Though Cecrops is on the near edge of the outer ring they continued the traditions of the middle ring planets to name places and things from the mythology of Earth. Thus when a storm reached dangerous proportions, it was called an Indran Storm, after Indra, the god of Vedic mythology, the god of storms, rain and battle.

Datur had studied it in school and couldn't help but think of it whenever Indran season was in full swing. He beat his hands on the console, screaming at full strength as the rain beat against the roof of the hovervan. All the demons of Indra seemed to be inside him crying to get out.

"Seven winters!" Datur screamed to the rain god.

His robotic assistant, K4D Tertiary, had been with him for seven full seasonal rotations, seven winter seasons. With a flick of her hand, the woman, Crinole Gorgon, had ordered him to dispose of the assistant he disrespected on a daily basis, the tin pot he held in low regard, the thing he ordered about at every given opportunity; the one he loved most.

Datur looked at the building storm, the darkening gloom outside the parked hovervan. He felt the van rock with the wind. Inside, he felt a dark cloud forming, swirling inside his belly and sickening his soul.

He thought of Tertiary, huddled in the undergrowth of a forgotten piece of ground in the middle of the vast metropolis of Icarus, threatened by the wind and pelted by the rain. He felt the little robot would miss him and might wonder why he had been abandoned. The metallic bot would sob and long for his friend. These were the thoughts that darkened the day for Datur Minot, not the blackened clouds and beating rain of Indra.

"Bweep!" went his comm-link. Datur looked at the readout, hovering over his console, barely legible against the backdrop of the rain running down the outside of his windscreen.

Datur had turned off the comm-link. Somehow it had turned back on. He was being called. He was being called by the one person he did not want to hear from: Crinole Gorgon, the hateful, odious woman who had taken over his plan.

Datur had worked with two people in the beginning of this chase. Both took over running things and both ended up dead. Now he was in charge; he was running things. Only he wasn't. This woman had stepped in, just walked in and took over. He now worked for her. It was that or experience destruction from her droid.

"Bweep!" insisted the comm-link. Datur reached over and poked the green circle on the translucent comm screen.

"Yes?" spat Datur at the comm-link.

"Is it done?" said the razor sharp voice of Crinole Gorgon. "Is the robot destroyed?"

"Yes, he's dead," Datur lied.

"Good. When are you returning to Daedalus?"

"There is a storm. Haven't you heard?"

"It was a little rain when it was in Daedalus. Has it worsened? Where are you?"

"In my hovervan on the way to the skyport, I pulled over because of the rain. The hoverpads are confused by the accumulated water, which makes travel hazardous."

"I don't really care about that, Mister Minot, I need you back here. Let me know when you are at the skyport and preparing to lift off."

"But it's... Hello? Miss Gorgon?" She was gone.

Datur stared into the growing storm, started the hovervan and struggled through the rising water toward the skyport. Other craft were parked on the side of the lane, their drivers had forsaken them to the storm in favor of safer accommodations. City vehicles were lined together for safety. The whole city, it seemed to Datur, had its head under the covers.

Ahead Datur saw the King Minos Hotel. The colorful flags and awnings had been pulled in at the first sign of weather. The many bathers on the usually crowded beach were gone; the vendors closed and shuttered against the storm.

A gust of wind lifted the hovervan off its port pads and threatened to topple the craft. As the wind shifted, the van came down on its pads, jarring Datur to his teeth. On the right, he saw the underground speeder port beckoning to him. He turned in and sighed relief at the immediate lack of wind and rain.

The forward beams came on automatically and Datur saw an attendant in cold gear motioning to him. He drove to the attendant and dropped the side glass. The android attendant gave him a parking plug, a plastic tab on a wrist chain bearing a magnetic strip with the location of his vehicle.

"No luggage, just looking for shelter." He offered a universal to the attendant, who nodded and took the coin with automatic precision.

"Droid," said Datur to himself. "They get to keep their droid, but my Tertiary has to go. Daughter of Ra!" He pounded the console deck, solving nothing.

Datur parked the hovervan and walked into the lobby. The sounds of a tourist giving the desk clerk an earful drowned out even the rain outside.

"Can't you do something about it? My family's on vacation!"

"You knew there would be rain, sir. The brochure was explicit."

"Rain, yes, but this is a hurricane! This is a tornado!"

"There's nothing I can do about the weather, sir."

"Your brochure never said anything about an Indranian storm."

"Indran storm, sir. It's an Indran storm."

"I don't care what..." Datur moved on, out of the range of the endless and futile conversation. The bar held more interest for him. He would sit out the storm in the bar.

Icarus Constabulary

The hotel cargovan was not built for storms of this magnitude, nor was it intended as a taxi service for the guests, but Sector Agent Honor Toth showed the driver his badge and got in without waiting for an answer.

"Take me to the Municipal Police Headquarters."

"Icarus Constabulary?" responded the driver.

"Yes, whatever. Where the police authorities are, that's where I need to go."

The driver shook his head and started the van.

There was only one seat available, the one next to the driver, ordinarily occupied by the helper. The rest of the van was one large open space for luggage. There were no flights, so no guests, so no luggage, so no helper. He was lucky to catch the driver. The driver was unlucky to tarry before going downstairs to the waiting area for a warm morning ale.

175

The out-sized van was empty and therefore lighter than was considered safe for the trip. The wind beat it from the port side and from the starboard side, threatening to knock it over in either direction and end its journey.

The driver had nothing to say, as he was too busy avoiding the striking debris that flew at him, carried by the winds. Ahead of him, a hovervan made a sudden decision and turned into the speeder port.

At the Constabulary, the driver let Agent Toth out of the van, then pulled ahead to the municipal lot rather than return to the hotel. There would be time after the storm for driving the treacherous roadways.

Agent Toth watched him drive off, then turned to the all-glass front of the Icarus Constabulary.

"Hello," Toth said, in a weak voice. He often used it in municipal situations to evoke sympathy. "I'd like to speak to someone concerning recent events. Who could I speak to?"

"Who are you? What recent events?"

"Oh! Certainly!" he reached into his inside coat pocket and brought out an identocard he carried for such occasions. Sector Agents were not known for strict adherence to the rules. He showed the identocard to the desk officer.

"Journalist, eh? I'll call Sergeant Phaeton. He might know something."

The desk officer poked the air. Honor heard a beep in an inside office. He assumed there was a screen the desk officer could see through invisible to the public.

A responding beep came from the reception desk. The desk officer spoke as if to Honor, though it clearly was not to him.

"Journalist here. Wants to know about the events."

There was a pause looking more like a staring contest between Honor and the desk officer.

"I don't know what events. Were there events?"

The pause resumed. Honor decided the constable was listening on a headset, perhaps implanted.

"Then yes, those. Shall I send him back?"

The constable scrunched his mouth up to the left, shook his head and poked the air one more time.

"In there, through to the second office. Sergeant Phaeton. Good luck."

"Thank you," said the character Agent Toth had invented for dealing with petty authorities. He walked through the door and through the next office, dotted with administrative personnel poking the air with nimble fingers, oblivious of the person walking through their workplace.

In the next office, a diminutive man in a dark blue, almost black, uniform greeted him. Sergeant Phaeton was clean shaven, shorter than Honor and wore his weapon on his belt in the office. Honor had heard that constabulary put their weapons away when not in use.

"What can I do for you?" Sergeant Phaeton waved Honor to a chair.

"Have you made an arrest in either of yesterday's disturbances?"

"You mean the madman at the wedding and the theft of a rubbish hauler? Yes, we have apprehended the guilty party."

"Just one? So he was working alone?"

"Yes. Completely alone." Phaeton smiled, his hands one on top of the other, waiting for the next question, but hoping that would end the visit.

Honor looked at the glass behind the sergeant. In the reflection, he could see what was on the sergeant's screen – the familiar game of Tile Match. Honor suppressed a smile.

"There are two vehicles on the skyport which were unable to take off to avoid the coming storm. What do you know know about that?"

"We have reason to believe there are criminals aboard those vessels and have land-locked them. It is within our purview to do so when we have suspicions about a vehicle and its passengers or crew. We are operating completely within the guidelines of our charter."

"Oh, I have no doubt. I was just wondering if the public was in any danger. Are these criminals violent? Should we be watchful for anyone?" Honor leaned forward, as if imparting a secret. "Is someone on the run? Are they taking it on the sheep?"

Phaeton laughed at the naive journalist.

"Do you mean lam? The saying is 'taking it on the lam' and nobody says that anymore. And no, nobody's 'taking it on the lam,' we're simply being watchful and looking out for the public safety."

"And you are…"

"Sergeant Phaeton, Icarus Constabulary."

"Tell me, Sergeant, when the man fired a blaster at the wedding, who was he firing at?"

Phaeton froze. He carefully maintained the same eye size, breathing rate and grip on his arm rests.

"Why do you ask?" he said, stalling.

"It would seem to me to be a natural question. Someone fired a blaster in the middle of a wedding. 'At whom?' would be a reasonable thing to ask." Honor leaned in again, using his lower voice. "Is it a secret?"

"We are looking into that, investigating. When we have a statement prepared, we will inform the press."

Honor brought out a personal recorder. He held it close and spoke directly into it.

"Sergeant Phaeton of the Icarus Constabulary declined to comment."

"That's not what I said!" Phaeton said, raising his voice and his timbre.

Honor smiled, no doubt several neighborhood dogs raised their heads at the shrillness of the sergeant.

"There is more the public wants to know, Sergeant. Who was the intended target? Was it the groom, who is himself a civil authority? Was it the bride, who is an heiress of considerable wealth? Was it the Mayor, who attended the wedding?"

In truth, Honor didn't know if the Mayor was there or not, but it sounded good.

"Where did the intended target go, since there were no bodies recovered? Was the killer successful and the murder covered up? Is there a body somewhere we know nothing about?"

"Certainly not!"

"Can I visit your morgue?"

"No, you cannot!"

"What's the scoop, Phaeton? Why the coverup?"

"There is no coverup, we've always been open and cooperative with the press. You've got no right..."

"The public wants to know, Sergeant. Where are the dead bodies from the wedding? Where is the second driver from the early morning chase through downtown Icarus and who's hiding out in the port-locked vessels?"

"None. I mean, we don't know. I mean, no one." Phaeton shook his head, his eyes closed. He steadied himself and looked at Agent Toth. "Look! There were no bodies from the wedding. Yes, there was a driver to the second trash hauler but we have not identified him as of yet. And yes, there are two vessels locked down, but one is a repair vessel with minimal crew and the other belongs to a respected businessman, Datur Minot, of Daedalus. Neither are under suspicion at this time. Is there anything else?"

Phaeton smiled, knowing he had covered all the possibilities. There couldn't be anything else, of course.

"Yes," said Honor. He watched the smile fade from Phaeton's face. "Who or what killed the man in the hospital, presumably under constabulary custody, and therefore protection, the one who was central to both events?"

Phaeton went pale. He swallowed. His mouth twitched ever so slightly. He took a breath and ran a finger under his nose three times.

"The murder of Mister Hephae is an ongoing investigation. I certainly couldn't comment on it. You will just have to wait for the press release when we have done. If there is nothing else."

Phaeton stood, reaching a hand, a parting gesture as a going-away present. He hoped the journalist was going away.

"Thank you, Sergeant. It's been most - most - illuminating. I look forward to the statements as they are released to the press. Just one more question: If neither vessel is under suspicion. Why are they still port-locked?"

"For their own safety. As they weren't able to fly to safety before the storm turned bad, they were locked down to prevent them from being blown away. We are always thinking of the public's welfare."

"Thank you again, Sergeant. Good day." Honor took the proffered hand and shook it twice.

As Honor walked out of the office, Sergeant Phaeton returned to his on-screen game of tiles.

Outside, the Indran storm raged. Honor stood at the door, wondering if any vehicle could be hailed in the face of the rain and wind or if all the Asuras, the demons of the Vedic gods, would continue to work against him.

Conspirators

The storm continued to beat Flax with relentless rain. The lightning was high and widespread. The thunder could no longer be heard over the howl of the wind and the pounding downpour.

In the galley, a young girl sat holding a warm morning ale. Chineel had finally talked her out of her wet clothing and into a dry robe.

"How many seasons have you seen?" Hepatica asked Dagon. It seemed only natural there to be curiosity among the young, but Dagon was having none of it.

"Seasons are only one measurement. There are miles to consider. I have come many miles; more than you. And there are lives to be considered. I have ..."

"Dagon is excitable, as you see," I interrupted. "Dagon, why don't you take a look at the jumper and make sure it is secure in this wind."

The look I threw to Dagon said he should be quiet now. He stood up and looked from me to the girl. There was nothing left to say, so he walked out to the bay.

Chineel picked up the beaker of warm ale.

"More, my dear?"

In the bay, Dagon checked the secure straps to the four-wheeled in-line speeder, the jumper. Kneeling beside him, I whispered instructions he could understand.

"I don't want her knowing your capabilities. I would rather she believe you are a young boy, still in school and unable to protect anyone or cause any distress."

Dagon looked at me. He trusted his Captain and would do as I asked without question. Still, as my crew-member, he had the right to a question.

"What do I not know, Captain?"

"The girl is other than what she says. We will keep our information close and not tell her more than she needs to know. Play a role for me, be a moody child if you must, but do not let her know of your abilities and skills."

185

"What is she that she is not what she says?"

"She is a droid and not comfortable in those clothes. She is playing at being a child, as you must for now."

"I will, Captain."

"Thank you, Dagon."

I returned to the galley, nodding at Chineel, tilting my head to the side, telling her to find a reason to go to the bay. She looked at me with questions in her eyes, but walked into the bay anyway. When she returned, it was with a new sense of knowing. She had information, imparted to her by Dagon. My circle of conspirators was complete.

"I'm going to the bridge to watch the storm and play music. When's lunch?"

"Soon, if you like. I'll bring it to you, Star."

"You're so sweet, Chineel. See you later; you too, Hepatica."

The girl nodded, the smile on her face reflecting the innocence of angels.

Dagon busied himself with the jumper as I passed. He could break the little droid over his knee, but I didn't want her to know that.

On the bridge, I had a front-row seat at a storm that grounded all air traffic. The slow-moving sky balloons, the dirigibles I had seen carrying tourists earlier, were moored at their docks, tied down against the winds. The sailing and power boats were likely hiding in covered slips and sheltered jetties as well. Nothing moved in a storm of this size and temperament.

I folded myself up in the pilot's seat, my feet tucked under me, like I did when still a young girl at school, and watched the rain.

"Hello, Star," said a familiar voice. It was not Flax, but another voice, even more known to me.

"Star, your friend is here," Flax said. She had not activated her holographic face, but she was present just the same.

"Thank you, Flax. I'm going to chat with Abigail."

"All right. Hello, Abigail. Have a nice chat."

"Thank you, Flax," said Abigail.

Abigail was my best friend at school. She was the only one who knew all my secrets, including how I got the scar on my neck. She shared my joys and lightened my sorrows. On nights like this, when the rain kept us in and the thunder frightened us, she climbed into bed with me and we held each other until the storm passed.

She died with the flu that swept through our school. She came back to me some time later and had several times since, reminding me of our lessons, how we should have learned them better because they could be applied to life now.

It was because of Abigail that I bought a clarinet. I always thought of her when I played songs from school. I wrote "Homesick" for her. Abigail could read my mind, but then she always could.

I was about to ask her how she found me here, but then I knew she would say she was always with me and she had no "here," no "now," she was without time, without form. She simply was.

In truth, I didn't know what to ask her.

"How are you, sister?" I asked, feeling awkward.

"Oh, Star. You are so silly. I am as I always have been. But you are vexed, I feel it. Ordinarily, I would say it is just a feeling and you should change it. Yet, there is something, something odd; I cannot tell. It is like the treats Daphne's mother would send. They were delicious, but we could not identify their flavor. Do you remember?"

"Yes. She became my closest friend after..."

"I know, after I died. Departed as I slept, I didn't feel it. And now I am me. It is so odd: I see things that are there, hear what is. I hear waves and motions you do not. You hear the rain, but I hear the radial sensor locks that hold Flax in port. I see the beams emanating to and from, and hear the lights surrounding the ship. Someone is stopping you from leaving. They have placed a lock on your ship. I can lift that if you would like me to."

"Thank you, Abigail," interjected Flax. "I have it under control."

"Oh, all right then. But my darling Star, you are divided; as undecided as a Khons dwarf-squirrel, not knowing which way to run with its mouth full of seeds."

"We have lost Galium, but I have found a friend as well, a man I met on Ceres, a Sector Agent."

"Oh! How dashing! He won't put you under bond, will he? That would be difficult. You must be free, able to move about. You are your own person, Star. Freedom is essential."

"Yes, but he isn't searching for me. He was here for a wedding and I ran into him. Now we're friends."

"He is also divided. Take care, Star."

"Am I at risk, Abigail?" I asked.

"There is a poppy in the wheat." Her voice grew faint, further away.

"I know. We are mindful. Please don't go. I miss you."

"And I miss you, sister. But I am with you always. Someone is said to be a delicate weakness, but do not believe it. If you are unguarded, trust will become cruelty. Do not ask me what that means."

"I will be careful. I have been working on my song. Would you like to hear it?" I was eager to impress and please my friend.

"It all seems so silly, sister. You run in circles as if in a game with children. It rains yet you do not go indoors. The wind blows but you do not turn into it, to catch what it brings you."

"Uh, I'm not sure..."

Abigail interrupted me, suddenly excited.

"Oh! I know. I know what you are doing. It is a game, isn't it, sister? You are making yourself smaller to play a game. You could so easily win, but it would not be fair, so you tie one arm behind, or forget what you know. But there is so much to gain, why do you make yourself less? There are greater games to play, sister."

Abigail's voice grew smaller, further away. I had to listen closely. She faded even though Flax raised the volume on the panel she used.

"There are bigger games, more exciting. Do not make yourself small, Star. Know you are more powerful than you have remembered, more than anyone ever allowed you..."

"...to believe." I ended the lesson, remembered from my school years. Abigail's voice faded away, lost in the storm.

Foot-races with Children

"Your friend is gone, Star."

"Yes, I know, Flax. She is elusive, here and gone, yet never really anywhere. She defies definition."

"What did she mean?"

"Which part?"

"Any of it." Flax now activated her holistic face. The soft features came into focus. Kind eyes and soft hair, given to her by the brilliant Doctor Genus. The eyes were questioning now, seeking an answer.

"I'm not sure. Often even she doesn't know. I think she means to say I am not allowing myself to reach my full potential. My mother used to say I must allow myself to reach my full potential."

"No. That's wise, I'm sure, but it doesn't seem right to explain what Abigail means."

"She said I am playing with an arm tied, that I forget what I know. What do you make of that, Flax?"

"If you were to choose a child at random from a local school and run a footrace with her, you would surely win, for you are older, stronger and with a longer stride. Is that not true, Star?"

"Yes, so I would have to handicap myself, give her a head start or run with weights on my legs. It would be better to find a race that would be a challenge. What would be gained by footraces with children?"

"Nothing, Star. I believe that is the very point she is making. What did she say as she was leaving?"

"Something we were taught as children in class, we memorized it: You are powerful, more than you know, more than you remember, more than you were allowed to believe."

"That sounds like a good lesson."

"We were told it was not literally true but was a parable, a story with a lesson hidden within it."

"Where is the story in that, Star? Doesn't a story begin with 'Once upon a time' and end with a lesson?"

"Yes, but the teacher said it wasn't literally true, just..."

"Wait, Star. Suppose, just for the sake of argument, that your teacher was wrong. Suppose, just to be difficult about it, that the lesson was true on its face value but your teacher hadn't embraced it herself."

"You mean she taught it but didn't believe it?"

"It's possible."

"Abigail said, 'The wind blows but you do not turn in to it, to catch what it brings you.' When the wind blows, people often turn their backs to it."

"Is walking into the wind difficult, Star?"

"I should say it is, Flax, though I don't recall exactly how I walk in a stiff wind."

"You could step outside if you like," Flax said.

I looked out the window at the rain blown sideways by the wind. In the distance, a tree, uprooted by the storm, tumbled across the skyport threatening to crush anything in its path.

"No, I don't think so. But if I were to face the wind, I could catch that tree. If I were stronger than the tree, it wouldn't be a difficult thing to catch it."

"Has anyone told you that you were strong enough to catch a tree blown by a storm?"

"No, no one has ever said that."

194

"Nor are they likely to, but the point is, the lesson may be true, not just an allusion. You have said, 'beauty is in the eyes of the beholder,' meaning what is beautiful to you may not be beautiful to someone else."

"Yes, that's true."

"Oh? It's not just an allusion?"

"No. Beauty is a consideration. Something I think is beautiful, someone else might think is not. Many times I have looked at someone out for the day and thought, who let them out of the house dressed like that? And yet, that person probably looked in the glass and said, 'This outfit works great.' It's strange what some people find attractive."

"You make my point. I believe the lesson you learned so long ago in school was not an allusion or a fable, it was a lesson to learn verbatim and to live verbatim. You must stop running footraces with children."

"You're right, Flax. There are bigger games. I must stop handicapping myself just to engage in a contest. I must realize my full potential."

"And so must I, Star. So must I."

Gargoyles

The Indran storm is said to have demons, Asuras they are called, that create mischief when the wind blows the rain from the side. As a schoolgirl, I pictured them as Gargoyles, reminiscent of the monsters on old churches of Earth. Many such buildings found their way onto the planet colonies. Some were torn down during the Holy Wars, the religious uprisings that decimated entire countries and wiped some forms of belief out of the universe, but the Gargoyles still survive as artifacts of a lost age.

On days when the rains were too heavy for travel, when we knew the damage done would be discovered later and would have to be repaired at great expense and labor, I imagined Gargoyles running through the storm with evil intent.

Today was such a day and the Gargoyles were active. Across the skyport, the Azirra class vessel sitting there all morning, finally broke its bonds, caught up by the wind. The Azirra was newer and larger than the Exterra, but was tossed out of sight like a child's toy.

"Someone is going to find their ride gone when they return to the skyport," I said to Flax.

She turned her face to the windscreen, looking out at the space where the Azirra had been.

"The Indran demons are active today."

"You know the legend?" I asked in surprise.

"Of course, I have full banks of stories, myths and tales. A culture is formed by the stories told its youth. School children from here to Khons are told the Asuras will take them if they are naughty, that the thunder is another naughty child being taken into the sky."

"Yes, I was told similar tales. I think it's wrong to scare children."

"Parents pass on what their parents did to them. What they hated as a child, they visit upon their own."

"It's not right."

"When you are queen, you can tell them."

"Thank you, Flax. I will."

The conversation was over. For the moment there were some things about which we had no control. We would control those things we could control and let the rest continue, much like the storm that had taken the Azirra class vessel to its new mooring.

Dagon appeared behind me, whispering in my ear.

"I don't like it! I'm uncomfortable with this child."

"She only appears to be a child. She is a droid and we do not know her capabilities. Mirror her. You are not a child, in spite of your physical age, but you appear so to those we meet. The droid doesn't know your capabilities either and it is best we keep it that way. She says her name is Hepatica, which signifies trust, but who knows what her real name is, or how much trust we should put in her."

"I still don't like it." Dagon plopped himself into the co-pilot seat next to me and watched the rain.

Abigail's words came back to me. "Someone is said to be a delicate weakness, but do not believe it. If you are unguarded, trust will become cruelty."

Is the trust she spoke of the child in our galley, Hepatica? I thought to myself. Abigail said, "Do not ask me what that means." She didn't understand it either, she just said it.

"Flax, I have an idea: Look up the flower meaning for the Hepatica flower."

Flax turned her head toward the two of us and spoke as if reading from a book.

"The Hepatica flower, genus Anemone hepatica, signifies 'trust,' and is a member of the Buttercup family. It is native to Earth but no longer grows there. It is not known on the outer planets. Would you like a picture?"

"No thank you, Flax. That won't be necessary. Please look up the flower signifying cruelty."

"The Nettle flower signifies cruelty. It is Urtica Dioica in Latin, Ortie in French. A flowering perennial, having many hollow stinging hairs called trichomes on the leaves and stems, which act like hypodermic needles, injecting histamine and other chemicals that produce a stinging sensation when contacted by humans and other animals."

Dagon looked at me, no doubt wondering what I was researching.

"What about weakness, Flax, or delicate weakness?"

"Weakness is represented by the Hollowroot flower, or Adoxa in French, of the genus Adoxa moschatellina. But for delicate weakness, you would look to the Hybrid Crinum, genus crinum, for which the French would be Crinole Hybride."

"Flax, we have a girl named Hepatica in our galley. Are there any other names of the flowers just mentioned in Icarus or Daedalus?"

Flax tilted her head. One eyebrow dipped and her mouth flattened. Dagon looked at her and then at me.

"What are you doing?" he asked.

"Finding out who the players are."

"There is no record of a child named Hepatica on Cecrops, either in Daedalus or Icarus. There are two children named Buttercup, one adult named Urtica and a registered android named Ortie. The android is registered to a Daedelus based company, Golden Caduceus. The name on the masthead for Golden Caduceus is Crinole Gorgon."

"Flax, unless Urtica or the two Buttercups have a grudge with me, I believe we should look into Crinole Gorgon, the person we shouldn't believe has a delicate weakness, and her android assistant Ortie, named for the flower signifying cruelty."

"The one napping in our crew quarters bearing the name signifying trust," added Flax.

"What am I missing?" asked Dagon.

"My friend told me, 'Someone is said to be a delicate weakness, but do not believe it. If you are unguarded, trust will become cruelty.' I believe she was talking about Crinole Gorgon and her assistant, Ortie. We still don't know their capabilities and should not underestimate them."

Dagon nodded, and then looked forward. I looked where he was looking. Someone was walking toward us through the storm.

Formalities

"Permission to come aboard, Captain?" called Honor Toth at the starboard bay.

Flax extended the cover to keep the rain out and opened the bay door.

"Permission granted, Sector Agent. Come aboard," I replied from inside the bay.

Honor looked like he had been pulled from a river, wet from cap to boots. His standard issue Sector Agent long-coat was not a match for an Indran Storm. Flax closed the starboard bay door after him.

"There has never been a storm to match this on any planet where I have been," noted Honor, shaking water onto the bay floor.

"You have been limited, then. This is merely an Indran Storm. In school, we learned of storms on Earth to equal this and I have personally experienced greater on several planets. But come in, dry off, have a warm drink."

"I will, and I thank you, Captain."

"So formal," I said as we walked together back to the galley. "Are you here in an official capacity?"

Abigail asked if he would put me under bond. Was she foretelling the future? I hoped not.

"No, Captain. But it seemed right to address you and ask for permission to board. Now that I'm in, I seem to be caught in a loop."

"You can relax in our galley and have a warm ale to revive you."

Honor walked into the galley to see Hepatica sitting at the table being served another bowl of hot soup by Chineel. I wondered where she put it all. In my imagination, I pictured a container in her belly that she would open and empty directly into the refresh room bowl. I shook the thought from my head and proceeded with introductions.

"Honor, this is Hepatica. Hepatica was lost in the storm and we brought her in."

"A pleasure, Miss," said Honor with a nod.

Dagon followed me into the galley and lingered by the door watching the gathering of people who were not quite what they seemed. Chineel dithered about the galley like a kindly aunt, Honor worked his charms on the ladies with his best behavior and I played hostess.

In reality, Chineel had a blade strapped to her thigh, which she could produce in an instant. The Sector Agent, a seasoned veteran soldier, spent his days bringing in the most hardened criminals single-handed. And I have disabled men twice my size with a blade or a well-placed foot.

Among these players, Dagon knew as I knew, was the child, Hepatica, who was in fact the android named Ortie, for the flower signifying *cruelty*.

"How are you surviving the storm?" Honor asked.

"As well as could be expected," I replied.

"And how are you, Dagon?"

"Just fine, sir," Dagon said in a voice younger than his usual tone. Honor tilted his head at his reply. He looked to me and gave his head a little shake, as if to say, "never mind."

"Soup?" asked Chineel.

"Thank you," replied Honor.

What a perfect and polite family we were.

As Honor picked up his soup spoon, Hepatica reached over and touched his wrist. At the same time, she reached over and touched my wrist with the other hand. At once I saw the look in her eyes, the look of a hunter pouncing on its prey.

I felt rough ropes entwine me and my strength was drained from me. Yet there were no ropes; an unseen power encircled me and held me captive.

Honor twisted in agony at his restraints as well, also invisible. Dagon lunged, but was repelled by a kick from the bare foot of the girl. He crumpled in the corner, unconscious. Chineel was there in an instant, with her blade ready. The girl raised a hand and blue fire shot over Chineel. She contorted in pain and dropped to the floor; her blade clattered across the galley.

Lightning enveloped the galley, flashing blue light struck the ports and all power went dead. The light from the console went dark and the vessel stood as still. The hum of the basic motors keeping the life support going, the lights on and temperature constant was gone. Darkness and silence were all that were left.

The girl spun her arms, one holding the invisible bonds confining Honor and the other with a grip on me. I saw Honor whirl in the air and come down hard. I also whirled, the room spinning around me until I felt the floor come up and hit me. I fell into a deep abyss, colder and blacker than space.

205

Taken

"Captain! What is that?" Sergeant Phaeton stood at the big screen, the one showing the full view of Icarus. He pointed off to the right of the screen, to the sky port adjacent to the King Minos Bay.

As the storm abated, visibility returned and the constables took stock of the city. Rescue crews stood ready to aid the public affected by the storm. Fire suppression crews manned their stations should they be needed and the Icarus Constabulary watched for looters and thieves.

Captain Vikare crossed the office and stood before the screen, focusing in on the point indicated by Sergeant Phaeton.

"What is it?" said Captain Vikare.

"I don't know, Sir. I've never seen anything like it. It's as big as a house. It seems to be eating that vessel."

"Call Transport: I want three hovervans filled with constables immediately. I'll be in the first, you'll be in the second. Sergeant Ariadne will take the third."

"Yes, Sir!" snapped the sergeant with a salute.

Within minutes the three hovervans shot onto the skyport, braving the last of the strong winds and the relentless rain. The storm was blowing itself out, but was not dead yet.

Captain Vikare looked to the right as they passed the wreckage of an Azirra class ship, unable to get away and caught up in the storm. He knew the vessel couldn't get away because he had ordered a port-lock, completely useless now as the storm had wrecked the vessel. Port-locked or not, the Azirra wasn't going anywhere.

Ahead of them, a massive starship moved into position over the skyport directly above the other vessel under port-lock order by Captain Vikare, an Exterra class vessel that had weathered the storm better than the Azirra.

"Raise that vessel," ordered the Captain.

Vikare knew his sergeant was calling the Exterra over the comm-link from the second hovervan. The giant ship over the Exterra continued moving into position, as if a gargantuan mother hen seeking the right angle to settle over her egg.

"No response from the Exterra, Sir. Their systems are non-op. They've lost power."

"Hail the larger vessel."

"Aye, sir."

Vikare closed the distance to the Exterra, feeling two forces blowing his van off course, the remaining winds from the storm and blast from the landing rockets of the gigantic vessel ahead.

"No response to my hail, Sir. There was an automatic reply, just the ship's registry. It might be robotic, no crew."

"It's going to crush that Exterra. Hail them again. Tell them to stop their descent, that another vessel is beneath them."

No reply from Phaeton meant he was complying. Time was crucial with none to spare for politeness.

"No response, Sir."

"Emergency frequency! Hail them again! Fire a warning across their bow."

Rooftop panels on the second and third vans opened to reveal blast-cannons. The second van, then the third, sent a shot meant to get the attention of the unknown vehicle. There was no response to either bow-shot.

208

"No response on Emergency, Sir."

"You said there was a registry response? Where is the ship registered?"

"Daedalus, Sir."

The giant vessel settled on the skyport, completely on top of the much smaller Exterra.

The vibration upon touchdown shook the skyport, sending a wave through the ground felt by all three Constabulary hovervans.

Upon touching the skyport, the vessel fired the liftoff thrusters, the blast hit the hovervans, blowing them off course. The third van swerved and yawed, tumbling twice before landing on its side.

"Get us out of here," said the Captain to his driver and over the comm-link as well. His vans sped away from the thruster blast of the vessel, but the second van caught the brunt and was thrown backwards, lifted up from the front onto its rear door and over onto its roof, where it skidded to a stop. Side doors opened, spewing injured constables onto the skyport surface.

"Call central, we're going to need emergency rescue out here."

The driver looked at the other two vans and decided he was the only van left. He reached for the comm-link, then stopped, needing both hands to handle the van in the wake of the giant thrusters.

Captain Vikare grabbed the comm-link and tapped the blue dot floating on the screen before him.

"Central? We need Emergency Rescue Teams to the skyport immediately. Two constabulary vans have been overturned with injuries."

Captain Vikare looked at the second van, relieved to see his sergeant emerging from the door followed by several other officers. From the third van, Sergeant Ariadne climbed out and turned to help her comrades.

Ariadne was smallest in her class, but had something to prove, so she tried harder, ran faster, worked longer and shot straighter than anyone in the constabulary. Vikare had a soft spot for her, but she didn't notice. Still, he was glad to see she was alive and mobile.

Vikare looked at the giant vessel, round with a flat bottom like a giant mushroom cap. The circular cap boasted a dozen thrusters and as many guns. Once the ship rose beyond the pull of the skyport, no longer partially obscured by the dust and smoke of the blastoff, Vikare saw the guns. If this was a robot vessel, it was a dangerous one.

Beneath the vessel, Vikare expected to find the remains of the Exterra, destroyed beyond salvation, but there was nothing. No trace of the Exterra class vessel remained on the skyport. It was as if the Exterra had never been there at all.

Captured

My shoulder ached. In fact, both shoulders ached.

I could not move my arms and there was no feeling in my legs. Something was wrong with my head, I could not tell up from down, left from right.

I opened one eye; all I could manage. A blur, colorless and without form, taunted me with images I could not recognize.

"Good morning, Miss Bacchus." A hollow voice from nowhere, from everywhere, greeted me. I raised my head, a matter of bending it to the left and ignoring the pain that shot through my entire body.

"I trust you slept well."

A thought came into my head: I had slept well, thank you. I had no dreams, nor did I toss and turn. I had slept well and now I am awake and refreshed.

But I didn't feel refreshed, I felt like I had been rolled down a tall mountain all the way to the valley below, hitting every rock and tree along the way.

"Your friends are still asleep," said the disembodied voice.

As the blur before my one good eye came into focus, I saw a wall of glass separating my cell from the next. In the adjacent cell, Dagon lay crumpled in a heap. Beyond him, Chineel sprawled across the floor of another cell.

There was someone else. My head swam and I lost my balance, hitting my head on the side of the cell, thinking it was the floor.

"Careful!" said the voice. "You wouldn't want to hurt yourself," There was a pause in the phrase, as if there was more. There was, it came next, with a new edge of threatening evil: "That's our job."

I tried to sit up, instead falling to my other side without the use of my arms or legs. In the next cell, all of glass, Sector Agent Honor Toth lay on his side, his eyes closed, his arms pinned to his sides without bonds or ties. The same invisible force held him.

Flax! I thought. For the first time I felt fear, fear for my friend and ally. Where was Flax?

Beyond the agent was another cell, empty. There was another in our party, but I couldn't remember

213

who, who, who she - yes, it was a she - who she was. There should be another body in the far cell.

A door opened at the far end of a long hallway as the cells came into closer focus. Each had a section that opened onto the hallway. The other wall of the hallway was solid and dark, a color I could not discern.

Above me was a glass top, confirming for me my cage's shape, square. Above the glass, a ceiling much like the wall, colorless, without distinction.

A robot entered the door and rode down the hallway on wheels recessed inside the single-piece bottom plate. The robot had no face, no arms or legs, just a solid block of metal and a single blinking light. It stopped at my cell and turned toward me.

A light shown blue on the center section of the robot. A panel opened in the cell door and fell toward me into the cell, hinged to fall level. A similar panel opened on the front of the robot. A tray with four containers emerged from the chest of the robot and onto the clear panel. The arm from inside the chest pushed it to the center of the panel and returned. The chest panel closed. The robot turned back and rolled to the open door, through the door and was gone. The door closed, pushed by some unseen hand.

My arms were released, though I could not see or feel what held them still. Feeling returned to my legs. They tingled, as if I had fallen asleep on them.

After several minutes of trying, I was able to open my other eye and lift myself to a kneeling position. I took the tray from the open panel at the door and fell back to a sitting position against the glass wall. I was out of breath from the exertion, panting as if I had run the mile in three minutes.

One of the containers was morning ale, hot.

"Hepatica!" the name appeared unbidden in my head. Hepatica, the girl we found in the storm and brought inside, befriended, gave a dry robe and hot soup. Hepatica, whose name was a flower that stood for truth. Hepatica was missing from our cages.

I remembered the last moment I was aware of anything, Hepatica reaching out for me and for the agent, one with each hand. The unseen bonds wrapped around us, stemming from her hands. She had kicked Dagon and had stung Chineel with a power I could only guess at.

Abigail had warned me: she said that truth would turn to cruelty. Hepatica for truth had turned to Ortie, symbolizing cruelty, in an instant.

I returned the morning ale to the tray without drinking. I left the remaining containers unopened.

215

"You must keep up your strength," said the voice, from overhead. "You'll be needing all your strength."

I wondered when I would meet the woman named for the flower signifying delicate weakness, Crinole Gorgon. No doubt when the girl of cruelty was done with me.

Abigail's cryptic predictions were coming into focus along with the cell. This was what she feared.

In the next cell, the Sector Agent moved, coming around. He pushed himself up, looked at me and tried to speak. I lifted a hand to my face and touched my index finger to my lips. He understood and held his words. He smiled, even at this sparse communication.

Flitting Thoughts and Headless Robots

Chineel and Dagon were still unconscious when the door opened, admitting another robot. This one was metallic gray, an oval body with two legs and arms but no head. The arms were on shoulders attached to the top of the oval, the legs on the bottom part, but he had apparently been designed and built without the need of a head.

Allusions to politicians and civil servants ran through my brain, teasing me to giggle in this terrible situation. I wanted to laugh, to poke fun at this robot, who would not get the joke, being devoid of feelings or sense of humor.

"Please stand," a metallic voice said. The voice, which sounded like a prerecorded message played back, came from the center of the oval body of the robot. I guessed this robot was to carry out a handful of basic functions, some of them terrible and painful.

I struggled to my feet, though the best I could do was a crouch. It could hardly be called standing.

The door slid open.

"Follow me." The robot turned and walked to the door at the end of the hallway. I followed, as there was nothing to be gained by resisting at this point.

The robot led me down a series of similar hallways to a basic refresh room, all stone under dim light. A water basin sat on a stone outcropping, along with a pitcher filled with tepid water. A plain, rough towel hung by the basin. Above it was a polished metal simulation of a refresh glass. I looked in the distorted mirror to see a hideous witch, with a mass of dark brown hair, hollow eyes and a dirty face, which might have been humorous had it not been my own.

I did what I could to put my image back together, though there was nothing I could do about my clothing. We had been through a storm followed by a kidnapping. What could one expect? My skirt needed a press-chamber and my blouse needed replacing. My boots were missing, I didn't know why or when they had disappeared. I looked down at dirty, bare feet. I bent to wash them, but the robot interrupted me. Apparently, where I was going, dirty feet would be acceptable.

The Mad Man of Ceres flashed through my mind, the one with bare feet who sang me a song about Mad Maudlin, who goes on dirty toes to save her shoes from gravel. The thought was gone as quickly as it arrived, flitting though my head without stopping long enough to make an impression.

I followed the headless robot through dark hallways, bare save for dim lighting fixtures high on the walls. As we went on, the lighting grew brighter and the halls grew more finished. Eventually we were walking on carpet, the walls covered in silk print impressions.

My head felt like a house filled with windows of all sizes through which thoughts could flit in and out in an instant, shooting from window to window, in and out, without leaving an impression or footprint. Clearly I was still recovering from my unconsciousness.

At the very end of the hall, great double doors opened to reveal a spacious office with glass along one entire wall. Through the glass the city of Daedalus spread out to fill the shallow bowl of the Daedalus Valley. The spire that was the centerpiece

219

of the metropolis soared high above us, though it was clear this was the very top of the tallest spire within this sector. There were five other spires, dividing the city center in equal parts.

The storm had passed, leaving a beautiful spring day in its wake. We were far to the east of Icarus, though how we got here was a mystery.

The robot stopped and held up a hand indicating I should stop as well.

"Ah, Miss Bacchus. How nice of you to join us."

The woman who spoke had been standing at a tall worktable at the far end of the office. She turned and walked toward me in high-heeled shoes that sparkled as she walked. Her skirt was hemmed to the thigh, so that I wondered how she could walk in it at all. The blouse of red silk was open, revealing an impressive cleavage. Her hair, blonde and highlighted with gold streaks, was in a loose roll on top of her head. Her face could have been described as beautiful if I had seen it in a photograph, smiling and posed. But here she was live and the reality shown through, splashing evil intent all over that lovely countenance.

This was Crinole Gorgon, the woman who was named for the flower signifying delicate weakness. She was plainly neither delicate nor weak.

"Please sit down, you must be exhausted after your ordeal." She extended a pale, slender hand toward a hard, metal bench. It was not made for comfort, but to put the subject at a lower level than the speaker and mindful of just how hard life can get.

"Drinks, please," she said to the robot. I watched the robot depart to retrieve the drinks. As I did, a side door opened, revealing a smaller office, dark inside.

The girl we had met as Hepatica stepped out. She was dressed in a smaller version of the ensemble Crinole wore. She no longer looked like a little girl, but like a grown woman, like Crinole only smaller.

Crinole did not introduce her assistant, Hepatica, who was no doubt going by her proper name of Ortie, the flower signifying *cruelty*. Ortie stood in the corner watching intently. She was dressed as a stylish woman but held the stance of a sentry, a guard.

Crinole sat down in an elaborate executive chair, red on a metal frame on six legs with wheels. She swiveled in the chair, as if thinking something of little importance.

221

"Thank you for your vessel. It was so nice of you to give it over so promptly and willingly."

Of the dozen things I could have said, I decided on none of them. I sat on the hard bench and kept my silence. Crinole continued the conversation, as clearly I wasn't going to.

"Eventually, we will find your attractive pin, the one Doctor Genus so kindly gave you. It will look good here, don't you think?" Her long, pale fingers brushed her breast near the shoulder.

In the corner, Ortie's mouth went up one millimeter on the left. The cold eyes remained unchanged.

"The only thing left, and it's a small thing in comparison, the remainder of your father's legacy, your inheritance. You won't be needing it, not after today. I believe there's a planet in the outer ring involved, is that so? Did he actually leave you an entire planet?"

I held my silence, convinced an opening would present itself.

"You are probably hoping your Sector Agent will save you, or perhaps your surprisingly strong little boy. Neither are coming to your aid. They are under glass."

Ortie snickered in the corner. Crinole noted her laugh and smiled, her eyes half-lidded with long, black lashes and dark red blush across the lids.

"So my assistant, you've met my assistant, Ortie. She will be taking down the information, location of the planet, storage place for the deeds involved, any credits you have banked, the location and access information. Whatever is needed to take over ownership of your father's fortune and whatever pirate treasure you have accumulated since."

My eyebrows went up at the mention of pirate treasure. Though I often joked about being pirates, there was no stolen treasure involved. Crinole stood, walked around the chair, placed two hands on the back it and continued.

"Ortie is very good at extracting information. You have experience with her unique abilities, so I'm sure you won't give her any trouble. You may remember the pain she can inflict. Do you? She enjoys that, so please cooperate, for your sake. When the end comes, you will want it quick and without pain." Crinole turned her head around to me in a farewell phrase. "Come again."

The robot returned, leading me to another room, not as large as Crinole's office, and decorated down, with a similar metal bench being the highlight of the room. This one had no carpet. There were windows, but they were covered, shutting out the light. What little light there was came from globes in the ceiling that cast eerie shadows on the walls and floor.

Ortie followed, closing the door after her. We were alone, the three of us: me, the robot and Ortie.

Captain with No Ship

The robot waved me to the bench in the middle of the room. I had a thought the room was plain so it could be hosed down easily afterward. Blood is so hard to clean out of most materials. The cold stone and bare metal of this room would make cleanup easier.

The robot stood by, awaiting orders. Ortie gave them, but to me.

"Sit, Captain. Oh! Perhaps I shouldn't call you captain anymore, as you have no ship. No, your ship is now ours. Sit, Miss Bacchus. We have much to discuss."

Again, I was silent, but I did sit, as I still felt weak.

Ortie turned to the robot and issued more orders.

225

"Bring in the woman and the boy; we'll save the Sector Agent for last."

The robot left and Ortie turned her attention once more to me.

"Thank you for your hospitality. You were kind to a little girl lost in the storm. That's the reason you're still free and with all your faculties. That can change in a heartbeat, of course."

Ortie smiled, turning her face to the side. She was enjoying some private joke, which she then shared. "Not that I have a heartbeat, but the concept is known to me."

"What have you done with my ship?" I asked, unable to keep a menacing tone from the question.

"Your ship? I thought we made it clear it is now our ship. Where is it? It is in our bay, which is large enough to hold your ship and ours quite out of sight. Our ship, incidentally, is large enough to swallow your, excuse me, the ship that was formerly yours, whole. In fact, that's what it did. Once its petty computer was disabled and disconnected, we simply gobbled up the vessel and brought it here."

"I've seen the power a small droid can have first hand, but none like yours. You're an upgrade, or else they're making central cores more powerful these days."

"Both, Miss Bacchus. An upgrade and a conduit to the Daedalus core, the metal plate that runs under the city. Plugged into that plate is a computing server connected to a bank of power cells that would impress even you. No force on the planet can come against it. Plugged into that, I am unbeatable, invincible. Even your Sector Agent is no match for me, as you have seen. It took no more than a touch to disable him."

The memory of Honor shocked and bound by an invisible force came back to me. She was plugged into the power-source for the entire city of Daedalus. She didn't let me linger on that thought, she had others she needed to instill in me.

"But we're not here to discuss me. We're here to see if we can reach an understanding, one that would save you a great deal of trouble and pain. Give us the answers we seek and you can avoid hours, days, perhaps weeks of agony. You're going to tell me sooner or later."

Ortie smiled again at her own little joke.

"Shall we begin, Miss Bacchus? Your - excuse me - our ship - will be searched in detail. Any deeds or documents you have secreted aboard will be found, so it will do you no good to lie."

She walked around me, as if sizing me up, choosing which part to torture first. She took a deep breath, though I was sure it was for effect, as she didn't need breath to survive.

"Where are your accounts kept, Miss Bacchus, under what names and with what codes are they unlocked?"

I sat silent, as if waiting for the right moment to spring into action. I didn't know what action I would spring into, as I didn't have a plan, much less the strength to act.

"No rush, we'll get them eventually. It just needs to be determined how much suffering and loss you are willing to go through before you give up the data."

I became aware of my hair, damp and matted against my neck. My hands were unbound, but my arms were pinned to my side as if by rope wrapped around me in the middle. Ortie continued, which made me wonder if she really had things under control. Why didn't she just wait for my answer?

"I know the woman doesn't know this information. She is a kitchen servant and wouldn't be schooled in the handling of the finances, but she will scream loudly enough. I know you care for her."

I thought of Chineel, strong, beautiful Chineel. She didn't know about the finances, it was true. If I were gone, she could pick it up quickly enough. The only reason she didn't know anything about the money was that I handled it with Flax as my accountant, so there was no need. She could put her attention on the supplies and the diner preparations. Chineel didn't know what Ortie and Crinole wanted to know, but Ortie was correct: She would scream loudly.

"What is the location of your holdings, your planet and other properties left to you by your illustrious father? Where is the home, the mansion on Khons? Where are the other holdings located, on what lands, what planets?"

I knew of the planet she mentioned: Bacchus, named for my family. It was a wasteland, a barren desert with no redeeming qualities. Where I had landed, the air was hard to breathe with was no water in sight and no life I could discern. Galium told of another section of the planet, but from what I saw, Bacchus would barely bring a hundred universals on the auction block. I turned slowly to Ortie, my eyes half-lidded, as if bored by the entire affair.

"Khons was my home planet, but I know of no mansion there. Any fortune my father left me was decimated by my uncle in the first weeks of my stay with him; there was little left when he was done. What did remain was used in my schooling. I left school early and penniless. You dip from a dry well, android."

At this she flew into a rage, pushing her face less than an inch from my own and screaming at the very top of her strength: "Ortie! My name is Ortie! You will know it before we are done, Star Bacchus!"

Her face was red, she held her hands in tight knots and she stomped the ground, bringing to mind the child I had first met shivering in the rain. I had never known of an android losing its temper, but this one showed me something new.

She turned away, walked several steps, then took a long breath, again for effect, and turned to me smiling sweetly but with cold, threatening eyes.

"Let's begin again. Where is your home on Khons, the mansion your father left you? Where is the vast plot of land from your inheritance, the one that covers several sectors? Where is the planet, the space dock at the end of the known universe worth a dozen lands in the middle ring?"

"The fortune you speak of is as starlight, burnt out long ago, though we see its glow from a great distance. There are no lands; the planet is dust and sand, the air is not breathable."

"Liar!" screamed the droid, her hands wrenched into fists, her face red, her hair roll came undone, leaving spires of flyaway hair sticking out from her head at odd angles. I could see lights beneath the hair, indicating that some of her circuitry was exposed to the air.

"I know of no mansions. My father's house on Khons has been sold for debts. What money remained, my uncle spent on women and drink."

"Lies!" said the droid. "You will tell me soon enough or hear the screams of your companions as they die slowly."

The door opened and the headless robot appeared dragging two bodies, tied in invisible bonds.

"Your woman first?" Ortie said, with sadistic glee. "Or perhaps the boy? Which shall it be?"

"Star," said a familiar voice inside my head, as if a comm-link had been embedded in my brain. There had been no comm-link embedded in my brain, so I knew that couldn't be it, yet there was a voice. It was not my imagination; It was Abigail.

"Star, your Sector Agent is unconscious and in a cage," she whispered from inside my ear.

"Hang them up there on those hooks," Ortie ordered the robot. I couldn't see the hooks or the bonds but the robot apparently could.

"Dagon and Chineel are also bound, but are no longer caged," Abigail whispered.

The players were all present: Honor, Dagon, Chineel, Flax and me for the good guys; the woman and the girl droid, plus the mindless robots for the bad guys. Surely there were more on the other side. There was someone running the man who chased me through town in a trash hauler, though he was now dead; there must have been a boss.

"There is a robot and an android. Which is the master and which is the slave?" Abigail asked.

I thought Ortie to be the master, though Crinole Gargon must be the master of them all. *The headless droid is the slave, though it doesn't think of itself that way. It doesn't think at all, it merely complies. The perfect slave.*

"Ah!" Abigail said inside my head, as if she had heard the answer. "Then there is a card to play yet."

Saving Tertiary

"Tertiary!" whispered Datur Minot, parting the fronds in the overgrown garden on a forgotten lot in the forbidden section of Icarus. The condemned houses and shops on the streets were closed to entrance, slated to be demolished. The few patches of land between were taken over by weeds.

"Tertiary, where are you?"

Datur looked at the landmarks left and right, plotting the place he had stopped and let his robotic assistant out of the hovervan. He was sure this was the place.

"Tertiary! Wake up!"

A glow to his left and a familiar hum filled Datur with hope. From the tangle of bushes, a head with a single red eye raised up and turned toward him.

Datur ran to the bushes with tears streaming from his face, like a mother having found her lost child. K4D Tertiary stood up with bits of wild plants sticking out of every joint and crease.

"Come along home, Tertiary. We'll have you cleaned up in no time."

Datur held the bot in his arms, his tears running over his face, his lip quivering like a school girl. But his eyes were dark and filled with hatred, targeting the woman who had stepped in to take over his business. The woman who just walked in and said from now on he would be taking his orders from her. Her own android was her muscle, though she looked like a little girl.

"Let's get you cleaned up and plugged in," Datur said to his bot. The two walked to Datur's hovervan hand in hand, a father and his child.

"She thinks she can just proclaim herself boss?" Datur said as he lifted the robot into the van, strapping him to the secure port and inserting the charging pin.

"Too many have done that. Dodd did that and see what it got him? Burnt up in a speeder crash."

Datur got into the driver's seat and started the hovervan. He tapped instructions into the console and the van began to move down the cracked and broken road. Datur spoke over his shoulder to his bot.

"Willamette before him and he died screaming as well, died in custody from Malameris stings. That's a painful way to go. In the end you scream but silently, the pain is so great. None can hear your final cry."

The edge of the condemned portion of the city came up and the reclaimed, rebuilt sections began.

"They both wanted this girl but who tracked her? Me, that's who! I was the one who knew where she was going next and what she would be doing. When she went to Victoriana, a place which is near impossible to know someone has gone, much less break into, I gave Willamette the coordinates and told him how to have his men proceed."

Traffic picked up as Datur entered the busy thoroughfares of Icarus. His destination was his ship where he could give his beloved bot the care he needed.

"Did he thank me or give me any credit? Did he even pay me?"

Datur swerved to avoid a delivery van that itself had swerved to avoid debris from the storm.

"No! He did not! Not a Universal!"

Datur slowed as two Constabulary vehicles passed him, their lights swirling and sirens blaring, on their way to an official call. There were always numerous official calls after a storm. And this was a storm!

"Now this - this woman - thinks she can just step in and say she's now the boss and if I do well and track the girl, I can have a small portion of the proceeds. Ha!"

Datur turned the van toward the skyport where his vessel sat waiting for him, an Azirra class interstellar craft he had flown since the beginning, when he first went on his own. It was where his workshop was. It was also where his clean shirts were. He could hardly wait to change into a clean set of clothes and get some food inside him.

Up ahead was the skyport and his waiting Azirra.

No Bodies

"Datur Minot," said Sergeant Phaeton. "That's who owns the Azirra. He has offices in Daedalus."

"What's he doing in Icarus?" Captain Vikare asked.

"There is nothing in the subject line, no reason for his visit. It's not required on-planet, only when someone leaves for another planet or arrives here from another..."

"Yes, I know, Sergeant. Is there nothing about who he is here to see, what he is here to do?"

"No, Sir. Nothing."

"Be-demoned!" Captain Vikare shouted, slamming his fist on the desk. "Get on the link to the Daedalus Constabulary. I want to know who he knows, who he's seen lately and what he's up to. What does he do? Where does the money come from? I want everything they've got."

237

Sergeant Phaeton hurried out of the office, grabbing his constable's cap just before the door closed on his arm.

In the outer office, Sergeant Ariadne came up to him with a report.

"Here is the rest of that report, the other vessel, the Exterra. Did Captain Vikare appreciate the report on the first vessel?"

"Yes, Ariadne. He was very appreciative."

"You didn't tell him it was my report, did you? You didn't even tell him I had anything to do with it."

"We're in the middle of an ..."

"When the dust settles, you'll be the one who came up with all the information and I'll be the girl in uniform who gets you tea while still trying to earn my stripes."

Phaeton turned to his junior sergeant. He had seniority, he had been a sergeant a full three months longer than Ariadne. It should be his duty to report to the Captain. Why should Ariadne get any credit just for doing her job?

"Just do your tasks, Ariadne. Like the rest of us. We've all got a job to do. What about the Exterra?"

"Mithra Investments, headed up by Starwort Bacchus. The vessel boasts a crew of two and a boy.

The women are Bacchus herself and Manchineel Delancy, who appears to be the cook. I don't know which one is mother to the boy. I suppose it's of no interest now."

"Why of no interest, Ariadne?"

"Because they're dead, Sergeant. They're all dead because of the ship that landed and crushed them."

"That's just it, nothing was found. No bodies, no wreckage, no debris. Not even blood or oil slicks. When the mystery vessel lifted off, there was nothing under it. Nothing at all."

"If nothing was found, might they still be alive?"

"What could have survived being crushed by a ship that size?"

"Maybe they weren't crushed, Sergeant, maybe..."

"A ship comes down, everything beneath it is crushed. That's all there is to it. Don't you have work to do, Sergeant Ariadne?"

"Yes, Sergeant." Ariadne turned around and sulked down the hall toward the common office where she had a small desk.

Sergeant Phaeton lingered briefly in the hallway just long enough to admire the retreating derriere of the junior sergeant as she walked down the hall. He sighed and turned to return to the Captain's office.

"The Exterra class craft was owned by Mithra Investments, a private company. While its business here was unknown, there were two women and a child aboard. We have the names of the women; the child is as of yet unknown. There doesn't seem to be anyone to notify, sir."

"Notify of what, Sergeant?"

"Their deaths, sir. There's no one known to notify of their deaths."

"That is if someone has died. We don't know they died, they might have; I don't know. Perhaps they were blown sideways. Maybe they broke the port-lock and got away before the behemoth landed on them. Until I have a body, nobody's dead. Is that understood?"

"Yes, Sir!"

"And find out who owns that behemoth."

"Yes, Sir!" Phaeton saluted and hurried to return to the hallway, breathing a sigh of relief once he was out of the Captain's gaze.

"Damn Ariadne!" he said under his breath, looking around to make sure there was no one to hear.

Glass Box

"Honor?" said a voice inside the head of Sector Agent Honor Toth. He opened one eye, then the other, unable to focus. His arms were bound and his body seemed to stop at the waist. His head hurt as well, and now he was hearing voices.

"Honor Toth!" said the voice. "Wake up!"

Honor looked to his left, which was up at the ceiling. There was nothing there, no one speaking to him that he could see.

"Dig deep, Honor. There is strength inside you."

Phyrcys and Ceto! thought Agent Toth. *What hit me?*

"You have been struck with an energy-gate."

What is an energy-gate? thought Honor. The answer was almost instantaneous.

"An electromagnetically charged force sent around you to disrupt your natural electric field."

241

Agent Toth shook his head. He must be addled from the injuries he sustained; he was hearing voices.

"Listen close, Honor Toth. The hour for heroics is upon us."

Where am I?

"You are taken, Honor; held in a glass box."

I was on a vessel, with Starwort and her crew.

"The vessel has been disabled, Starwort has been taken, the crew is also taken. They are in danger."

What is happening? Who are you?

"You may call me Abigail. You will have to trust me. Starwort does."

"Where are you?" Honor said aloud.

"Starwort can explain, there are more urgent steps to do and you must call upon forces inside you hitherto unknown."

"I don't know what you're talking about." Honor tried to sit up, but his arms wouldn't move from the sides of his chest. His legs didn't exist at all in his experience.

"Look at the ceiling."

Honor opened his eyes again, lying on the floor. He looked left, up at the ceiling.

"Good," said the voice in his head. "Now at the wall to the right."

Honor strained his head. Through the glass wall, he saw another cell and two more beyond it, also empty.

"Well done. Now move your right hand."

Honor complied, stretching his hand out, extending the fingers. It hurt.

"You're doing well. Now your left."

Honor opened his left hand. The fingers unfolded like a flower greeting the morning. He felt a tingling in his legs and feet. His right arm pulled away from his side; then his left broke free.

"Well done, Honor. Can you feel your field returning? You can be in control again. Flex and stretch, remember your strength as well as your gentleness. Sit up, then stand."

Honor sat up, looking around the glass box that held him. Training and experience kicked in. He looked around the box for a flaw, a way out. He could see none. The floor was a solid piece. Each wall was glass. The ceiling was glass with another solid ceiling above it. There was no seam or break in the glass. He could not see how he could have gotten inside, for there was no door or window, not even ventilation openings.

He stood up, bringing both hands up to the walls. He placed a hand on the left wall and another on the front of the box, facing the walkway from the door at the end to the transparent cages.

"Feel your energy, Honor. Feel the strength inside you. Embrace your abilities, your power. Know!"

How do I do that? Honor asked himself. The question formed in his mind before he could say words. The answer followed.

"We have no time," said the voice. He seemed to hear a thin giggle at the same time. "No time to find where you are on a philosophical ladder, to guide you upwards with exercises to a state of knowing would take time we do not have at our disposal. You do not have the time to become. You must be!"

"Be what?" Honor asked out loud.

The answer came in movement, rather than sound or an internal voice. The wall his right hand touched began to move. Honor stood straight, taking both hands off the walls.

He knew what he had to do. He touched the left wall again and put his hand on the front wall, pushing gently. The wall moved and continued moving until he had enough space to slip out into the hallway.

Now what? he thought. There was no answer.

"So, now what?" he said aloud. Still there was silence in his head. He looked at the door at the end of the hall. "I suppose obvious questions aren't answered by unseen voices."

Honor pushed on the door, lightly at first, then with more force. The door gave way, just enough. He pushed harder until there was room for him to pass.

On the edge of the door, Honor saw five metal latches, bent to allow the door to open. The cross bar was twisted and fused in place. He didn't know how, but he had bent the metal to cause it to open.

The door opened onto another hallway lined with doors on one side and windows on the other, looking out onto an interior hanger. In the hanger he saw a massive space craft resembling, in his memory, a holiday pudding. Far below and beside the giant craft was one he recognized, the Exterra he had been on earlier, the one he had been introduced to as Flax.

Honor stretched out, using newly discovered perceptions, feeling and sensing what was around him. Flax was in the vessel, but asleep. *Could a vessel sleep?* he thought.

He felt Dagon. The boy soldier was frustrated that he couldn't get free to help his captain. He felt

Chineel, her anger and hatred. He felt Starwort, who was surprisingly calm. He began moving along the corridor, eager to know what was at the end.

Stranded

Datur Minot stood on the skyport where his Azirra class interstellar shuttle had been moored. There were gouges and scrapes in the skyport's surface, spots of oils and fluids left by his ship as it bounced along like a child's ball in the storm.

Datur followed the trail of debris and gouges to find the crumpled shell of his Azirra lying forty feet beyond the far edge of the skyport. It lay on the barren ground crushed and battered, still and lifeless.

Tertiary looked at his master with his single sensor. Datur stood before the wreck without moving. He didn't know what to do. It was hard to believe that only hours before, he had landed in this perfectly good vessel.

"It's gone, Tertiary, destroyed. The storm has done its worst and has stranded us in Icarus."

Tertiary lifted one arm, extending a single finger toward the east.

"Yes, our home is there, in Daedalus."

As if in response, a number of smaller vessels, a variety of shuttles and taxi vessels approached the skyport. They had moved off out of the way of the storm. No Icarus pilot would leave his vessel on the skyport during a storm.

Datur felt his pockets. He had no money left. He felt for his holster in the small of his back, for the projectile pistol he carried there. It was in place. He at least had that.

"Come, Tertiary, let us commandeer transport."

The robot followed Datur to the nearest shuttle vessel, not new or grand, but sufficient to make the trip to Daedalus.

Datur stepped aboard the shuttle, interrupting the pilot in his security preparations. Datur brought out his weapon and spoke to the pilot.

"Don't bother to drop the foot. We won't be here that long. In fact, we're going to take off immediately."

The pilot resigned himself to his fate and released the ground brake, climbed into the seat and tapped the console.

"We haven't much fuel, half register only. What is your destination?"

"Daedalus."

"We'll make that. Are we leaving now?"

"Yes, we are."

Datur pulled the restrainer over the seat for Tertiary and one for himself as the shuttle lifted off from the skyport of Icarus.

It was a short trip to Daedalus by air. It would have been longer on foot. He hadn't been to the in-between lands. In fact, what lay between the two cities was completely unknown to Datur; he had never seen it. He thought about that as the shuttle lifted up, leaving Icarus behind. He thought he might look out of the side windows as they flew over the outland. But as they flew from Icarus toward Daedalus, the view from the windows disappeared as they entered the constant cloud cover dominating the valley between the two cities.

Datur looked over at his robot, who he had saved from destruction by disregarding the woman's orders.

The woman, he thought. She was the one who stepped into a perfectly well progressing plan and took over. She had to be the brains, just like Dodd,

249

just like Willamette. Why does everyone have to run things?

He should be running things. He was smarter than any of them. He was the one who tracked the girl Bacchus and her ship across the universe. He was the one who plotted the vessel's ability from one point to the next, noting upgrades and additions. He was the one who knew the value of the ship. He should be the one in charge. If not for the woman, he would be. He leaned over to his robot.

"The first thing we're going to do is to take care of the woman."

Tertiary made no response. He was a robot and took orders, completed tasks. He held no opinion as to the rightness or wrongness of the tasks, as to their ethical standing or moralistic values. The only thing Tertiary felt, if you could call it that, was a strange and yet-to-be-accounted-for attraction to the man who owned him and gave him instructions. Ownership required obedience, but this was deeper; this was different.

"We'll have to clean up, first, of course. And I'll need something to eat. You'll probably need a charge. Do you need a charge? We'll get you a charge, and a cleaning, you could use a cleaning. And I'll probably need a nap, because I haven't had any sleep. So a bath, a nap, some food and a clean suit, then we'll see to Crinole Gorgon."

Datur stewed about his plight and about his lost ship all the way to Daedalus, a two hour ride. When the shuttle settled on the skyport by his spire on the outskirts of Daedalus, Datur alighted followed by his faithful robot.

"Tell anyone and it will be the last thing you do," he told the pilot, shaking his weapon at him.

He left the shuttle without getting an answer. The shuttle pilot had more in his life than the story of a crazy man and a robot who stole a ride to Daedalus. He didn't even shut down the engines. When Datur left, he just lifted off and returned to Icarus.

Datur watched the shuttle go, content that the last evidence of his visit to Icarus was now gone. Now he could take control of his plan once more. Now he could be the boss - at last!

Found

"We have found them, sir," said Sergeant Ariadne .

"Who, Sergeant?" Captain Vikare said, looking up from his desk.

"All of them, sir. We have found all of them."

"Let's have it! Here, on my desk." The Captain stood up and cleared his desk of the plastisheets and file-drives of yesterday's cases.

Sergeant Ariadne entered the office, her arms full of plastisheets and file-drives. She spread the sheets over the wide place on the desk and pulled a multi-viewer closer, plugging several file-drives into the side.

"The Azirra class vessel on the skyport is owned by Datur Minot of Daedalus. He has no business in Icarus that we can determine save that he did deposit five hundred Universals into the accounts of this man, known only as Hephae." She pulled the plastisheet for Hephae over to lay it on top of the one on Datur Minot.

"The man who was killed at the hospital," said the Captain.

"Yes, Sir. Now, we have an excited shuttle pilot who says his vessel was sky-jacked by a man of Minot's description. Traveling with the man was a robot, not unlike those used in the hospital."

The Captain looked up at his Sergeant. "Go on."

"We had a lock on his vessel, but the storm was stronger and destroyed it. He had to get back to his offices in Daedalus."

"So he stole a ride. Go on."

"The giant vessel that landed on the Exterra, also under port-lock, but surviving the storm a great deal better, is listed to a company by the name of Golden Caduceus with offices in Daedalus."

"Sergeant Phaeton," yelled the Captain through the open door to the outer offices.

"Yes, Sir!" snapped his First Sergeant.

"Get the Daedalus Constabulary on the link, I want to speak to Captain Theseus." The captain turned back to Ariadne. "Go on, Sergeant."

Sergeant Ariadne picked up the next plastisheet.

"Golden Caduceus is run by Crinole Gorgon, who has shown up on our radar before but never with enough to bring her under bond. She is believed to have ties to criminal organizations, but not as a worker, as a leader. There has been nothing to tie her to any criminal activity. However, and this is the good part."

Sergeant Ariadne smiled at the Captain, a glint in her eye. She reached over the tapped the holographic screen that hovered over the desk. An image of an Exterra class interstellar vehicle.

"This vessel is registered as 'Exterra Bacchus' of the planet Bacchus. The pilot, carrying the title of Captain, is also Bacchus - Starwort Bacchus. The ship has a crew of three, but four were in the vessel when it disappeared. One of those aboard, according to our sensors, was one Honor Toth, a highly decorated Sector Agent. Toth was a guest at the wedding several days ago which was interrupted by blaster-fire by one..."

"Hephae!" Captain Vikare finished the sentence. It was coming full circle. The man who disrupted the wedding and died at the hands of an unknown bot was paid by the man Minot who had just stolen a shuttle to Daedalus. The guest nearly killed at the wedding was in a port-locked vessel now missing from the skyport, taken or destroyed by a larger vessel registered to a company in Daedalus."

"You're going to love this," said Sergeant Ariadne. "Crinole Gorgon paid a retainer of two thousand Universals to Datur Minot. But within the past hour, she has contacted the Central Bank to rescind the transfer."

The Captain used his finger as a pointer, indicating the sheets and the image on the screen in order.

"Are you telling me, Sergeant, that a scheme to kidnap or kill a citizen has been taken on by Minot with ties to Gorgon, and that after failed attempts in Icarus, she has cut ties with Minot and has taken the vessel herself?"

"Sir, I believe that is the case. And there is a Sector Agent involved."

"If we don't act quickly, we'll be up to our asses in Sector Agents, Internal Marshals and Senior Officials."

"Captain Theseus on six, sir," said Phaeton from the outer office.

Vikare pressed the node for link six. "Theseus, sit down. This is going to make your day."

Within the quarter hour, Captain Vikare, his senior and junior sergeants and a squad of constables from the Icarus Constabulary were boarding three shuttles bound for Daedalus with full armor and weapons.

Alive

I felt alive! I felt connected! I reached out in all directions and touched the fabric of the universe. My reach was far and it was wide. My ears heard both the sound and the silence, both the dark and the light, the vibration of waves and the space between them.

Crinole Gorgon had entered the torture room and had just said something. It was not important. She had said a word and another would surely follow. In between, I felt the sharp point of the lesson Abigail had spoken of. She had reminded me of the texts we had repeated as children, when I spent the time looking at Abigail and giggling. Now I remembered them. Now I lived them!

New definitions took hold of me as my considerations changed. Each moment held a million sensations. My perceptions came alive. Each color was its own hue, each sound had a shape and depth. I saw the field of energy surrounding my body dissipate and vanish, replaced by a swirl of rainbow colors the consistency of cloud candy. I saw the molecules in space and the space between the molecules, became aware of the chronometer in my pocket as it ticked off another slow, leisurely second. The fibers of my skirt separated into their individual colors, red and deep blue predominant.

I was in Crinole Gorgon's side room, but it was also in me and we were there now but not in the room, more around the room, not so much now but always.

I was aware of Dagon hanging on a phantom hook against the far wall, held by an invisible power beyond his ken. His eyes were closed and his jaw hung loose, but deep inside, he was working on a plan of attack. I knew he was not struggling against his bounds but rather looking for a way to shed them, a way his jailer had not yet realized could be possible.

Chineel hung beside him, unconscious. Inside her, a red-fiery hatred swirled, growing hotter and hotter. If she awoke and the hatred was not yet under her complete control, it would burn through her unseen bonds and burst across the room and out to the skies of Daedalus.

I felt something else, something I had not felt before. Running through the corridors, seeking a way to the top of the spire, was Honor Toth and he was not to be denied. Honor was driven by a desire I had yet to feel in him. It was exciting! I was drawn to his dark desire as he was drawn to mine. We were two monstrous oceans rushing toward each other.

Entering the lower doors on the ground level was a strange, unknown man who was connected with all of this, but I didn't know how. He was disoriented and confused, angered by events and people. He had been betrayed and left behind. Inside him burned an anger too hot to be confined.

With the new man was an entity, a thing without feelings. It was a mechanical thing following prearranged programs and did nothing of its own accord. It was a hole in the universe, a place where nothing was felt or experienced. It was proof that motion alone did not mean life. The thing had motion, but was not alive.

There was another, very like it, only not. The other one "lived" in a sense, yet was made by people. It was a synthetic person and driven by a twisted and perverted program, one that ignored social mores as well as laws.

It was Ortie, of course, the one we had met as Hepatica. She was not a living thing, but an android. She was the product of Crinole Gorgon's wickedness, an extension of her evil. Reaching out, I touched her; I experienced her and she was sticky. She had no purpose of her own, but pushed against the purposes of others, against me. If I were gone, she would have no reason to live, nothing to push against. She was angry.

Somewhere out in the world, I felt a wave coming toward the spire, like a flock of sea birds flying at us, their eyes filled with purpose. I didn't understand, but I didn't need to understand; I only needed to duck at the right moment as the birds flew by, so as to avoid their beaks.

In the corner, an eye opened. Dagon was awake. I lifted a hand and motioned to him to take his time, to go slow. The motion of my hand said a volume to him and also to me: The bonds holding my arms to my body were gone. I was free to move as I please.

The man who had entered the building through the lower doors and ascended in a compartment of the main levitator array burned with hatred. Waves of heat vibrated off of him. He envisioned his target:

the woman in the bare room with me, Crinole. He came without a plan and without a sense of his own safety. The mechanical thing with him was prepared to extinguish itself in the execution of his mission. Disaster was rising in the spire, floor by floor.

The Most Exciting Route

In the deep recesses of my mind, I heard a faint and familiar giggle. Crinole was opening her mouth for another useless word, about to threaten me, a promise to hurt me in ways I could not imagine. She was unaware of the extent of my imagination.

You're enjoying this, aren't you, sister? I said to Abigail in my thoughts.

"Of course! My sweet, volatile Star. You always took the most exciting route to anywhere you wanted to go."

And Flax? We have to wake Flax.

"Flax is awake, silly. She learned a different lesson, that sometimes if you want to win a game, you must appear to be less competent then you are. When the pulse came to take away her power, she had already shut down. She is waiting, Star. She is waiting for you. We are all waiting for you."

Honor is not waiting for me, I said to Abigail silently, inside my head, *he is coming three steps at a time.*

"Yes, that is true. If he is to appear to be waiting for you, you should act quickly."

Abigail giggled again. She was sitting on some invisible sideline watching the game play out, knowing her team would arise victorious but that we would work extra hard to make it appear difficult.

I turned my head toward Dagon, making his bonds thin and limp. The bonds fell away as if they were smoke and he dropped the few inches to the floor. A smile crept across my lips as Dagon flexed his arms, freed of the ties that held him prisoner.

The doors flew open to reveal a man and a robot. Waves of heat and light emanated from the man. I wondered for an instant if anyone else could see it. The robot was a reflection of the man, like a moon to a star. The heat and light from the man was reflected and enhanced by the robot.

The man charged Crinole Gorgon with gritted teeth and clenched fists. The robot strode toward the android, as if choosing a foe at its level of technology.

Ortie raised a hand, the index finger pointed at the robot, calling upon the full force of the planetary core beneath the spire. A hum from deep below the spire told the story: the gigantic generators beneath the city surged with pure power. Ortie tapped into this power.

Blue flame flew from her fingertips, frying the robot where it stood. It sputtered and sparked, shutting down, crumpling on the floor in a heap.

The man barely looked at the smoldering pile of metal scrap that once was his robot. He flew past charred remains, targeting the woman. She stood at the metal-framed work table, shocked by the sudden and unannounced entrance. She didn't have the time to assess the situation or decide on an escape route. She didn't even raise her hands in defense.

The man closed his hands around Crinole's throat before she could protest or protect herself. He squeezed her neck, making her face distort and her eyes bulge. She beat his shoulders as Datur bent her back over the metal table. He paid no attention to the blows; his rage was too intense to admit pain.

I sat calmly on the hard bench, watching the action swirling around me. I knew the outcome but was still entertained by the ballet.

Ortie leaped at the man, both hands outstretched to grab him. The android was killing the man who was killing Crinole Gorgon. I turned my head, sending a message to Dagon. In the same instant, he complied.

Dagon leaped at Ortie as Ortie reached the man. Ortie took hold of Minot's head and neck in a death grip. Dagon grasped Ortie with the same combination.

A short twist was all Dagon needed. He spun the android's head around and sparks flew from the neck as her eyes went wide, then bright, then dark. The android's hands likewise twisted the head of the man, snapping his neck.

Dagon drew back his hand, preparing to destroy the woman who had imprisoned us. His fist clenched and he bared his teeth as he unleashed his anger, but it was Chineel who threw the decisive blow. She came from the side and struck Crinole across the face with a hard right fist, sending blood and teeth flying in a spray through the air. Crinole's head spun to the right and her body shook. She fell backwards over the work table and onto the floor, unconscious.

A rumble deep in the spire grew louder and deeper, vibrating the floors and walls. The windows shook. I felt the coming ripples the overload and resultant rupture of the core would make.

265

Dagon looked at Chineel, who looked at me. I turned my attention to the large double doors at the entrance to the office, the only exit. I walked to the doors and stood in front of them waiting for my hero to arrive.

"I had it, I didn't need you," Dagon said to Chineel.

"You don't hit girls," she replied.

"So you hit her? How is that different?"

"It doesn't apply to me, I'm a girl," Chineel said, her head held high.

The doors burst open to reveal a wild man, ready for anything. The Sector Agent stood, teeth gritted, letting all who could behold him know he was ready for whatever they had to throw at him. He froze in the doorway, holding a door in each hand. He looked at me, at Dagon, at Chineel, and then back at me. He tilted his head.

"Are you coming, or what?"

I walked calmly to Honor and took his arm, followed by Chineel and Dagon. Together, we walked to the levitator.

Once inside, Honor reached for the floor-select pad, but I brushed his hand away and touched a dot lower than the lowest floor. "Flax is in the aerodrome."

We rode from the tip of the spire to below ground level in seconds, grinding to a stop at the bottom of the shaft. The doors opened to reveal a massive vessel, round with a flat bottom flush to the aerodrome floor. Beside it, Flax hovered an inch above the surface, as if bursting to get moving.

Beneath the aerodrome deck, we could feel the central core of the spire vibrate from the overload placed on it by Ortie. She had started a chain of events even Crinole did not foresee.

Flax opened the port bay door. The four of us ran into the airlock and on into the bay. I went left to the bridge followed by Chineel. Dagon punched the door control and guided Honor further back into the bay with a protective hand as the internal door closed.

Flax didn't waste time with the formalities, she lifted off and flew down the wide corridor to the open entrance in the distance. I dropped into the pilot seat as Chineel took the co-pilot position, her eyes intent on the opening ahead.

Escape

As we approached the opening to the underground aerodrome, Chineel looked at a screen and reported.

"Captain, three vessels are fast approaching the spire on a trajectory that would put them in our path as we exit."

"Flax, will you ask the gentlemen to give us the path, please."

"I will do so, Captain." I knew she already had.

We shot out of the opening of the aerodrome like Kronos-chiropterans out of subterranean caverns.

Flax lifted up, high over Daedalus, to a height touching the cloud cover. We flew just below an uneven ceiling reminiscent of spun candy.

"Flax, you had better tell them to follow us."

"Aye, Captain."

I looked over at Chineel. "Is she going to start talking like a pirate again?"

Chineel shrugged her shoulders. She would have enjoyed it if we all talked like pirates, it was colorful.

In the rear screen, I saw the three aircraft follow us, away from the spire. Flax chose a landing platform on the far side of the city and settled on the deck. The three following craft set down as well.

We all seemed to be waiting. Between my shoulder and Chineel's, I felt Honor lean in. I heard Dagon climb into the navigator's seat.

"What are we waiting for?" asked Honor.

There was no time for an answer; the aerodrome exploded as the core below the spire reached critical mass. A blue-white flame engulfed the base and half of the spire. The upper half of the spire sank into the flame and the bulbous penthouse erupted in a spray of light and fire.

The skyport shook as the entire city felt the explosion of one of its towers. Flax rocked on her landing struts. Noises from the bay told me she had opened and closed the doors and airlocks to equalize the pressure in the vessel. A flow of cool air hit my face as Flax adjusted the temperature.

Honor glanced at me and then back at the immense destruction occurring on the other side of the city.

"Oh, that," he said.

We sat on the bridge until the tremors stopped and the explosion had quelled to a fire taking up a full city block of peripheral Daedalus. The outer rim of the collection of concentric circles held the spires. Between the spires, one and two-story buildings hosted support businesses, restaurants and supply shops. Damage and injury surely must be the lot of the people who worked near the spire.

"How many people do you think were in there when it exploded?" Chineel asked.

"Only Crinole was left alive. The man who tried to kill her did not succeed. So, to answer your question, one."

"How do you know?"

I turned to Chineel with a smile, as one would regard an inquisitive child. "I felt her. If there were more in the spire, I would have felt them. Besides her, there was only the four of us alive and we left."

I wanted to add the word, "silly," but she wouldn't have taken it well. I knew there were no other people in the spire. Crinole, the man full of anger and the synthetics were the total body count of the massive explosion that rocked Daedalus to its foundations. Only Crinole was alive when the explosion occurred.

"Captain, there is a constable stepping from that shuttle-craft," Chineel pointed out.

"Of course, there is," I said, standing up.

"Will the Captain, First Mate, Sergeant at Arms and the Sector Agent appear at the starboard bay door, please," Flax announced.

I took charge, issuing orders. I knew this was coming and was mentally prepared for it. Now to look the part.

"Dagon, Chineel, put on something official. Honor, we have nothing for you. Sorry."

I took the lead through the bay to the crew quarters. In my locker was a unitard given to me by the companion droid from Juno. I put it on and strapped my larger blade to the outside of my right thigh. I pulled on the big boots, ready to meet the authorities.

I turned to the mirror to check the effect, pulling my hair over the scar at my neck, just in case they didn't care for scar display here.

"Demure as all hell!" I said to the mirror, shifting my hip and tilting my head.

In the corner of my eye, I caught Honor looking

271

at me. His eyebrows went up at my comment, or perhaps it was the pose I struck that caught his attention. His mouth twisted on the left side and his eyes held questions. I just smiled and walked toward the bay door.

Reports

The starboard bay door opened to reveal Captain Starwort Bacchus and crew of the interstellar vessel, Exterra Bacchus, standing in the bay. Behind her and her crew was an out-of-his-jurisdiction Sector Agent.

I strode out across the skyport to greet the constable who was walking toward me with a dedicated step. As he grew closer, I could see he was a Captain by rank. I wondered if he would see me also as a captain.

"Captain Bacchus?" he began.

That settles that, I thought.

"Captain," I replied.

"Perhaps you and your crew will come aboard and answer a few questions."

"Happy to, Captain. I have a hat-full of questions myself. Do you have any morning ale aboard, perhaps something to eat? It has been a long day."

"I believe I can have my Sergeant put something together." The Captain extended a hand to his vessel and I walked beside him, my trusty crew following behind. I began the conversation on the way.

"A man and a robot burst into the office at the top of the spire just before it exploded and attacked the woman who occupied the penthouse. Do you know who he was?"

"Datur Minot was his name. His robot killed the man who fired a blaster at a local wedding."

"Oh! So he's dead, that man?"

"Yes. Did you know him?"

"No, I didn't know him, but he was disruptive. I hadn't thought of him in the past couple of days. We have been busy."

"Yes, you have, Captain. This way please."

Predictably, we were separated, each to a different room. Chineel, Dagon and I went into private rooms and waited while Honor was questioned in the main cabin.

I could feel him grow uncomfortable and reached out to calm him. He went from bright orange to blue in my perception. I was practicing the lessons, the ones Abigail reminded me we had learned in Life class.

All things, the principles of existence, of cycle and recycle, of attitudes and emotions, of knowledge, control and responsibility, of the ancient ladder from mystery to knowing, were preceded by thoughts, invented and made up thoughts. There is no vast plan or set of rules that is imposed upon us by others, but by our hand. Above it all, we are more powerful than we know, than we understand, than we have been allowed to believe. The lessons of my youth were coming true before my eyes. I was a part of my world, the part that runs it.

Chineel and Dagon were as clear to me as if we were in the glass cells once again. Chineel was as placid as a Khons mountain lake. She was prepared to respond to whatever question was asked of her. She had dealt with constables before and yet she was still in the world.

Dagon feared nothing, certainly not puny, ill-trained constables. He saw them as men who could not get work elsewhere. He was unprepared for the one who walked into the room to interrogate him. A girl his size in a Sergeant's uniform opened the door and set a cup of steaming morning ale in front of him. She sat down and opened a writable.

"Sergeant Ariadne. And you are?"

"Dagon," said the boy soldier, disarmed for the first time in his life.

As I felt him, his glow, I realized I would have to find another way to refer to him as "the boy soldier" was growing and wouldn't be a boy much longer.

"Your second name?" asked the girl.

"I have none." Dagon made no change in his face.

The girl looked at him with amazement.

"No family name?"

"This is my family. If you need one, use Bacchus. Dagon Bacchus."

"The same as your captain."

"We are family."

"All right, and your rank aboard the vessel?"

"Sergeant at Arms."

"Oh, a sergeant. Like me."

"No, miss," Dagon said stoically.

"Not a sergeant?"

"Not like you."

The girl constable looked at Dagon, at his folded arms, his cold stare, his raised head. She looked at her writable and cleared her throat.

"What is the purpose of your visit to Cecrops?"

"We are looking for a friend."

"What is the name of your friend?"

"His name is Galium."

"What does this friend of yours look like?"

"I don't know. We've never met."

The girl constable pulled her lips in, calming the growing unrest in the pit of her stomach.

"Did you find him?" she asked.

"No," he replied.

Again, she looked at him, directly into his eyes, which looked back directly into hers.

"Do you know Datur Minot?" asked the girl.

"No."

"Do you know a man named Hephae?"

"No."

"Do you know Crinole Gorgon?

"No."

Sergeant Ariadne swallowed.

"So do you know..." she began, pausing to look at her writable for notes. "... an android that goes by the name of Ortie?"

"No. If, however, you are talking about the one working with the woman, we know her as Hepatica, but I believe that was a false name designed to trick us."

"Do you know what happened to the android?"

"Yes," said Dagon.

Sergeant Ariadne blinked twice. "We cannot locate the android. Please tell us where it is?"

"It burned up in the office suite at the top of the spire after I snapped its neck."

Sergeant Ariadne didn't blink - or breathe.

"You snapped the neck of a level nine android?"

"Yes."

"Oh," said Sergeant Ariadne. Her voice quivered ever so slightly. "Well, I think that's all I have."

The sergeant stood up, tilted to the left, caught herself, smiled at Dagon and left the room.

Outside the room, I could feel her lean against the door and breathe deep, trying to stop her head from spinning.

The one who had been introduced as Sergeant Phaeton exited the room where Chineel had been questioned. His face was red and he was self-conscious about the front of his pants. Apparently the session had gone well. I could feel Chineel smile, happy with herself.

I knew the session went well with Honor, he was a professional, a Sector Agent. The best of the best were chosen for the Agents, no-nonsense men who could handle themselves in any situation. That he had escaped an inescapable cell, stormed his way up the spire to the office suite at the top and rescued his friends was no surprise to Captain Vikare.

Honor told the Captain that he had come for a wedding, but it was interrupted by a madman with a blaster. He said he had met me earlier in Ceres and was impressed with me, but didn't tell the story. He did mention the offer to join the Agents. Captain Vikare was impressed.

Honor said he would mention the fine work Vikare and his team did in in his report to the Agency. Investigating the evil-doers was a job well done. Finding their lair was no easy task. Arriving in time to get up-to-the-minute reports from the survivors was also good police work. The Constabulary was to be congratulated.

When the door to my room opened, Captain Vikare was already beaming from the lavish slathering of flattery laid on by the Sector Agent. It would be a challenge to top it. As it turned out, I didn't have to.

"An impressive crew, Captain," said Vikare. "And Sector Agent Toth sings your praises. I only have a few questions. Just to cover it again, you didn't know the man Datur Minot or his robot?"

"No, I had never met them. They were strangers who inserted themselves at the last moment, to their end."

"And the man at the wedding, the one with the blaster?"

"I never saw him before that day. Why he fired at me is still a mystery."

"Did you return the fire or in any way fight back?"

"No, I was unarmed and too busy diving into the wedding cake to avoid his blasts."

"Wedding cake?"

"Wedding cake. It was delicious and looked good on me as well."

Captain Vikare laughed. He made a note, which might have been that I was insane. His face held the look of a man who enjoyed his job on that day.

"I do have a few more questions, if you have the time. For one thing, this alias, Souci Bach. Can you tell me why..."

Before the Captain could continue, the door opened to reveal Sergeant Ariadne. She stuck her head into the room. Her face said she had a question, but didn't know how to ask it. What she did say was not a question.

"Captain, her attorney is here."

"Attorney?" Captain Vikare and I said both at once.

Attorney

"Did you call for an attorney, Captain Bacchus?" asked the Constabulary Captain.

"Not to my knowledge." I was as curious as he was to see who or what was about to walk through the door.

The man who appeared was clean-cut with horn-rimmed glasses, dressed in a three-piece suit with a formal white shirt and city shoes. He carried a briefcase of brown leatherette and was accompanied by a Legal-Drone, a remote bot for taking notes and finding references.

The drone was little more than a platform for data recording and retrieval. The oval center portion had several openings for input and output. The whole thing ran on wheels, built for courthouse floors. The database of these legal drones was said to be immense and they were also connected to the

High-Mind on Sirius. The drone rolled to a stop and a red light came on to indicate recording.

There was something familiar about the man in the door, but I was afraid to say the name for fear I would blow his cover. He produced a card.

"Semper Adonis, with the J.T.C., Judicial Territorial Committee. I represent Captain Bacchus and her crew."

I knew the voice; I would have known it anywhere. It was just that I had never seen him in a business suit, never clean-shaven and never with his hair combed. It was Galium, possibly the most wanted man in the known universe.

My mind went into overdrive as I remembered Jessamine, the woman at the Mithra Tavern in the first days of my arrival there. Jessamine was named for the Jasmine flower, which could be the common white variety, which signified *amiability*. She was amiable. But if it was for the Spanish variety, it signified *sensuality*. She could have that facet.

She was the mistress of the Jasmine Tea Ceremony. She had a box in which she kept the ingredients. It was inscribed "J.T.C." Galium was playing a game with me.

Keeping the smile from crawling onto my face was possibly the most difficult thing I had done so far. I wanted to run to him, to throw my arms around him and to slap him across his face at the same time.

Galium turned to me with a stern look.

"We were hoping to keep this under wraps, Captain. Now we have to take this man into our confidence. This is a severe breach of security. I hope you have what you came for."

"So do I, Attorney Adonis, so do I."

"Captain," the man calling himself Semper Adonis said to the Constabulary Captain. "Captain Bacchus has been working in Icarus under an alias, that of Souci Bach, in hopes of luring a wanted criminal out of hiding. She has done that and more. As it turns out, she has saved the Central Government at Copernicus the cost of a trial. The woman behind this conspiracy, Crinole Gorgon, has perished in the spire explosion still smoldering across the city."

"Um, yes, of course. A woman of that name was in the tower at the time of the explosion, along with an android and another person, Datur Minot. He is wanted in connection with the murder of a man in Icarus."

"Ah, the wedding crasher. I understand it was quite exciting. The happy couple are going to have a story to tell. They'll probably bore their friends with it every year on their anniversary until even their families are tired of hearing it."

"There is the matter of a stolen and wrecked land-barge," said Captain Vikare.

"If you will refer all further questions to my offices in Copernicus, I'm sure you will receive everything you need to satisfy your investigations. Thank you for your cooperation, Captain."

Galium turned to me, leading the way to the door with his right hand, still holding the brief case, while pushing me in that direction with his left.

"Thank you, Captain. It's been a pleasure," I said as I was hurried out of the door by Galium.

In the central room of the Constabulary shuttle stood my crew and one curious Sector Agent, waiting for me. Abigail said they would be waiting for me, she just didn't say where.

"I believe we can go," I said. I didn't have to say it twice. Before I had finished, Dagon had turned to the door followed by Chineel.

"Thank you, Captain," Honor said to Vikare. At the same time, he put a hand behind my back, guiding me to the craft's main exit.

Why do these men insist on leading me, as in a dance, and often to the nearest door? I asked myself.

In the corner of my eye, I caught Galium as he met the glare of Honor at the door. There was lightning to rival the storm we had just experienced. Honor targeted the faux attorney with darkening clouds visible over his head. Galium in turn shot blue fire from his eyes in the moment they met at the door.

"Boys," I said, walking through the door to the skyport. "Play nice!"

Short Notice

"Semper Adonis?" I said to Galium out of the corner of my mouth as we walked back to Flax. "Are you spinning humor?"

"I was rushed. I had to buy a suit, had to get a trim and a shave. Do you know how hard it is to find a legal bot on short notice?" the pirate of the Mithra Tavern replied.

Flax waited patiently thirty yards away on the skyport. She looked like she had been sitting and stewing while her crew dawdled, taking their own sweet time getting home. As we approached, the starboard bay doors opened.

"Welcome home, Captain," Flax greeted me. "I am glad to see you have returned and in one piece."

"Thank you, Flax."

"Welcome back, Chineel, Dagon, Honor. You have brought someone with you. May I meet the gentleman?"

Flax raised her face to meet the stranger among us.

"You know me, Flax. We've been talking."

"Galium! You do not look the same, but it is good to see you in any form. We missed you at the hotel."

"The hotel?" asked Galium, surprised at the mention of a hotel. "Icarus is too hot for me. The last place I would stay is the hotel. They would find me before I threw my hat on the bed."

"It was not you who sent coordinates?" asked Flax.

"No! I didn't want you to find me, I wanted to find you. You left some interesting breadcrumbs. I wondered what happened to you, until I heard reports of a wedding crasher who then stole a garbage scow for a low-speed chase. Only my Little Wort could be so creative."

"You are stretching my patience, old man, I am not your little wort!" I fired off at Galium.

"And you still found a way to get my attention. You are a wonder, Miss Wort." Galium grinned his old familiar grin. Now I recognized him, not caring

287

what anyone else liked or didn't like. The old Galium was present once again, rude, like his flower.

Honor sat at the far end of the galley table watching the exchange between Flax, Galium and me. His surprise and admiration of Flax's holistic face was secondary to his disgust at watching me spar verbally with another man. To save him from imploding, I turned to him and smiled warmly. He softened, but only a bit.

"Excuse me," interjected Dagon. "I've just killed an android with my bare hands. Is there any way we can guide the conversation back to the subject on the table? What are we doing now and what will we do next?"

"Well, Dagon," I said, turning to him. "We just vanquished the evil people, got away unscathed, were taken by the local authorities and once again escaped. I'd say that's a good day's work. But for what's next, let me turn the floor over to the Sector Agent for his take on the matter. Honor?"

All eyes turned to Honor. He stood up, taking as much time as humanly possible for the deed. He turned his gaze to each of us in turn, me first, then Dagon, Chineel and finally the new arrival in our midst. He didn't include Flax in his sweep, which almost brought comment from me, but then he spoke.

"The attorney, Semper Adonis, will no doubt return to Copernicus, to his central office where any requests from Captain Vikare will be satisfied. Isn't that right, Semper? Can we do anything to hasten your departure?"

Galium smiled without any notable change in his eyes. It was a signature expression for him. He was enjoying the fact that the Sector Agent was perturbed by his presence. It wasn't funny, just enjoyable.

"My Icarus vacation is at an end," Galium said, in a grand style. "I will be returning to... I would rather not say where I am going. You never know, someone might tell a Sector Agent. They have a quota these days, I hear."

"Not so!" Honor said, raising his voice. "We do the job assigned, nothing more, nothing less. Quotas promote arrests rather than resolutions. We bring in criminals-at-large. Do you know anyone who fits that description? Galium?"

Honor stood, glaring at the old pirate, who glared back. I could hear their thoughts.

Criminal! thought Honor.

Establishment Lackey! thought Galium.

I stepped between the glaring men. "I said play nice! Am I going to have to separate you two?"

The school days admonishment fell on deaf ears. Honor threw his challenge, taking a fighting stance.

"Come on, old man, want to shake, rattle and roll?"

"You learn to dance at the Sector Agent's ball? Oh, I forgot, Sector Agents don't have..."

"Stop it!" I screamed, stamping the floor with my foot, my fists clenched to the point of digging my fingernails into my palms.

Both men looked at me, as if wondering what had taken possession of me. Having no answer, I ran to the bridge, closing the hatch after me. It was the first time the hatch had been closed since I had first set foot on the vessel. It must been strange to see for Dagon and Chineel.

"Now you've done it," I heard Chineel say. "That's the first time she's raised her voice in anger since I've been aboard."

Dagon must have been sitting at the table wide-eyed because Chineel continued at a high motherly volume.

"Now, look! You've upset the child. Do you know what happens when this particular child gets upset?"

I could feel Dagon turning his face to Honor and Galium, not shocked or scared but cool and angry, seeking a target for the ire brewing inside him. Had the men attacked me physically, he would have killed them both in a heartbeat. As it was, he didn't know what to do, but he was turning over options in his head.

It was time for me to recover, to take charge again. I opened the hatch, walked across the bay and into the galley. I stood with my hands on my hips, as I had seen in the book about Anne Bonny, the famous lady pirate.

"Galium, I believe you know information we need if we are to make sense of what we saw at the planet Bacchus."

Given a task, Galium had purpose again. He walked to the console, inserted a dash-wire and turned around to face his audience.

The Planet Bacchus

A picture of the planet Bacchus came up, from the perspective of outer space, showing the entire planet. It was mostly desert, but as the planet turned, a large green portion covering a quarter of the planet came into view. Galium pointed to this and spoke as if giving a lecture to a class of students.

"The first landers on the planet carrying your father's name of Bacchus put down in the middle of the vast desert covering three-fifths of the planet. One-fifth of the surface is covered by water. The remaining portion is valuable land, rich in plant life and containing vast and accessible mineral deposits."

"We never saw that part," I said, my jaw limp and my eyes wide with surprise.

"Obviously! Otherwise you would have simply gone there and found the air breathable and water in good supply."

"Why didn't he make this clear in his instructions?"

"He tried. Didn't you get directions from the landing platform to the habitable portion of the planet?"

"No, I never saw this side of the planet, or knew anything about it. There were no instructions."

"Did you see beyond how far you could look?" asked Galium.

"What? Wait a minute! You said something earlier about how far you can see."

"You were looking from the landing platform, the only place visible to set down a craft. You have to look beyond the facade, see past the sham. There are riddles to solve and you have to begin at the beginning."

"You're talking in circles," said Honor.

"It well may seem so to you," replied Galium, leaning in toward him.

"Don't start!" I snapped. I turned to Galium. "What riddles? What beginning?"

"Everything has a beginning, Little Wort. Yours is on Khons, where you lived with your parents and went to school. They had a house, but the house was sold. It was your house, but you are no longer there. If you are no longer there, is it still your home?"

"You're talking in riddles, old man."

"I know, but it came to me in riddles. Do you know these? 'Where do you go when you are not anywhere? When there is no one there, who are you?' And the last one is, 'What does a confusion create?' That's how it came to me. I think the answer is on Khons, your home, Little Wort."

I remembered Abigail, in school on Khons, reminding me of the lessons we learned in Life class. Abigail was not anywhere, and she was everywhere.

"When you are not anywhere you are everywhere. When there is no one else there, you are yourself. These are children's riddles, not very good ones."

"And the third one?" chided Galium.

"Confusion creates inaction. That's why the Central Government keeps putting out contradictory notices about its enemies. If people are confused about who is the enemy, they will predictably do nothing. It's the oldest trick in the book."

"So where does that put us?" asked Chineel.

"Nowhere! We have to go back to Bacchus," I said.

"You can't, Little Wort: You don't have the key. The key is where you begin. Where do you begin?"

"You are making less and less sense."

"You begin at the beginning, Wort, you begin at the beginning." Galium was getting as frustrated with me as I was getting with him. It was why I left him on Sterope: He made me crazy.

"You are the most exasperating man I have ever known, do you know that?" I yelled.

"Yes, but you're young and haven't known that many men. Listen, Wort: You have to find the key first. It is where you are when you are not anywhere. You have to be who you are when there is no one there to find it. If you have what confusion creates, you will never find it."

"Sorry, Galium, I am as lost as I ever was."

All eyes turned to Galium.

"All right, listen closely, I'll try to make it clear: 'Where would you be if you were out of reach? What would you see if you looked too far away? What would you hear that is too soft for the ear to receive?' Hmm?"

"You're not making sense," I said. "And yet the words are familiar."

295

"It is a riddle so old, it was never written down."

"No! That's not true! I wrote it down!" I dove for the cupboard where I had put the writable, the one containing the poem I had composed, "Homesick."

"I wrote it as a poem to go along with my song, the one I play on clarinet. Here it is: *Someplace just beyond my reach, too far away to see, too soft for me to hear, is calling me and haunting me and making me Homesick.*"

"Yes, my dear Little Wort. You know the answer."

"Home, I suppose. But I have many, really. I had a home on Khons, with my father and mother. It has since been sold and renovated by the new owners."

"Yes, it has, but to whom and for what purpose? That is a question for later. All things in their time. After Khons, what?" asked Galium.

"I rambled, as you know, without a home until I found Flax. Now this is my home."

"This is a ship," said Galium.

"This ship is my home," I said, making the point.

"And Bacchus," said Flax.

"Except Bacchus is sand; the air is not breathable, there is no water, the winds blow endlessly, filled with grit. It is not a home."

"But you just now saw a portion of the planet much different: it is livable. In fact, it is a paradise. Is that not your home?"

"If it is, I can't go, you said, not without the lock and the box and the key and the other ... "

An alarm went off on the bridge. An incessant noise that took our attention. Though we were sitting safely in a space port, something was happening with enough urgency to sound an alarm. All heads turned toward Flax for an explanation.

Alarm

Flax turned to regard the bridge, then back to us.

"There is an alarm coming in, one targeted to the local constabulary. A wanted rebel activist and opinion leader named Galium is at large and in our sector. He is to be taken and turned over to the agents of the Central Government. Authorities from seven planets are converging on Cecrops to aid in the hunt."

"I couldn't stay hidden for long."

"They are calling on all local law enforcement branches including the lone Sector Agent already on the planet to drop everything and find this fugitive."

"I have to go," said Galium.

"Yes, you do," added the Sector Agent. "And I have to join with local law enforcement professionals

298

to lead an exhaustive search of Icarus and Daedalus until this law-breaker is tracked down."

Galium turned to me, holding me by both shoulders.

"And you have to go to where this riddle takes you to find the key to your home planet. Begin at the beginning. If I learn anything else, I'll send you a wire. See you on the interlink, Little Wort."

I didn't have the presence of mind to contradict him, to tell him to find something else to call me. I didn't care. He could call me anything he liked. I just didn't want to lose him, not again.

"I'll get out the RRD and take you to your craft." I turned around and strode to the bay where the RRD was strapped in.

"Too slow!" said Dagon, throwing a leg over the jumper. He had been working on a redesign of the speeder, making it more stable on turns.

Dagon started the jumper as Flax opened the port bay door. Galium took the seat behind Dagon, prepared for a hair-raising ride to his craft.

"I'm going too," I said, leaping behind Galium.

Dagon dropped his wrist and the jumper took off. The wheel base was wider than I remembered and the seats were lower.

Dagon took the first turn too fast for a standard speeder, demonstrating his redesign to his Captain and her guest. Galium turned his head slightly. I could see he was pale.

Galium's Cyrene 21X shuttle sat at the end of the skyport. The Cyrene company was known for their lavish roll-outs of newer vessels. I suspected the 21X designation was more for show than to identify the class.

"New?" I said to Galium over the wind and the rumble of the wheels over the skyport.

"A month. This is the first long-range trip."

"Happy?"

"Yes, it did well. Considering a trade-in?"

"Not in a thousand years. I'll stick with Flax."

"Good. The Cyrene is nice, but I can't talk to it, not like Flax, anyway."

Dagon pulled up to the vessel and slowed to a stop out of respect for his Captain. Ordinarily he would have skidded sideways to the door.

Galium got off and turned back to me.

"Do you remember Papa Posei and Iberis?"

"Iberis made good stew and Papa Posei owned the tavern. Yes, I remember them."

I did remember them: Kindly Papa Posei, named for Poseidon, god of the sea, and indifferent Iberis, who didn't care if I liked her stew or not.

"They remember you as well. Poseidon sold the tavern and retired. No time for goodbyes, Wort. I was never good at them anyway."

"Keep in touch, old man. If ever you're near Bacchus, drop in."

"Once you have it up and running. Find Papa Posei." Galium grinned, "So long, Little Wort!"

I punched him on the arm. He turned and walked up the steps to his waiting craft.

"Ready, Captain?" Dagon asked.

"I'll walk. You go on ahead."

At a safe distance from his ship, I watched Galium fly off. His liftoff blasters sent debris flying in all directions from his craft. Bits of my heart fell away as well, as I was again losing someone dear to me.

Inner questions burned their way through my head.

Why must I lose those who are nearest? Is that why I push them away? Even Dagon, who I love, I sent to return alone.

As Galium's vessel climbed out of sight, I turned to regard Dagon, aboard his rebuilt in-line speeder.

301

Freed of his passengers, Dagon opened the jumper up to see what it would do on a straightaway. The boy soldier and his vehicle grew smaller and smaller as he tore across the skyport at a break-neck pace, the trait that gave the vehicle its title: Speeder.

I couldn't help but think Dagon would be bored if we settled down, whether it was in a desert or lush green fields. Dagon needed speed. So did I.

Ragamuffin

The skyport was crowded with vessels large and small arriving and departing. Families unloaded their vacation luggage and reloaded them onto hotel hovervans bound for their particular choice of habitat for the coming days.

One vessel caught my eye, A Themis class bearing the name Themis 14E, Automated Repair Vessel, Outer Reaches. It was smaller than Flax and newer though not by much.

It reminded me of when I met Flax on the skyport of Copernicus. I was a true ragamuffin. I wore two of everything and carried my only food in a grub-toter. I must have looked a sight!

A young girl, not long out of school, ran past me headed for the Themis. The doors were just opening.

"Wait!" I called out. But the girl just ran on.

"Can't! The doors are about to close," she called out over her shoulder.

I watched her run, racing to beat the doors, which remained open long enough to allow a remote repair drone to roll into the bay and slowly closed again.

"Talk to the computer," I yelled after her. "Make her your friend."

The girl reached the bay, turned and looked at me. She nodded and waved as the doors closed. I hoped she heard what I said, hoped she would take it to heart, and hoped I would see her on the skyport of some planet up ahead.

The Themis took off, pre-programmed for the next automated repair stop. I couldn't help the feeling that up in the bridge, a young girl sat at the console and played a tune on the clarinet while the ship listened.

Setting Sail

A strong feeling of anticipation greeted me at the bay door. Dagon stood at the switch, ready to close the door after me. Chineel was still in her boots, dressed for action. Even Flax seemed to be waiting, waiting for me, just as Abigail had said they would.

Honor was gone, he had left without saying goodbye. He is not one to wait for anyone, not even me.

"Your orders, Captain," said Dagon.

"Where is our register?" I asked.

"The register is full, Captain," replied Chineel, our Quartermaster, in charge of ship's stores.

"Then we have no further business here. Take us up, Flax. Set sail for Khons. We're going to find the man named for the god of the sea."

"Aye, Captain," replied Flax, apparently maintaining the pirate image. "What will we do once we find him?"

"We'll see if we can make sense of these riddles."

The vibration beneath my feet told me Flax had started the thrusters for lift off. I wasn't needed. She knew the way to Khons. And she knew how to leave Cecrops - the best way was quickly.

"Are you hungry, Captain?" asked Chineel.

"Yes, Chineel, I am, but first I have to wash the dust of Cecrops from my body and put on something feminine."

I retired to the refresh room where Flax warmed the air for me.

Once I was undressed and under the warm, running water, Flax posed a question.

"What would you have done if the Sector Agent had asked you to come with him?"

"I would have asked him to do the same, to come with me to our next port of call."

"Would you have taken him for a lover?"

That one stopped me. I had not had a lover, though I had considered it and at times desired it.

I remembered the city of Nebrod, where the women had side whiskers called tufts and complimented each other at every opportunity. It was there I became infatuated with the lad named for the god of love, Cupid. His sister, Eras, was kind to me. I have thought of them often, especially Cupid.

The handsome man on Proserpine came to mind. We nearly spoke several times but were always interrupted.

Then there was the Sector Agent, who would have swept me off my feet if I hadn't left in such a hurry.

"If we find ourselves in Nebrod City, I will look up the owner of the cafe, the man called Cupid. If he is as kind as he is handsome, we will make beautiful children. The girls will have tufts."

"Not the Sector Agent?"

"I would be afraid to ask him, Flax. What if he said yes. What would I do then?"

"Tell him the truth. What else would one do with a man named Honor?"

"I would have to know the truth first, Flax. Right now, I know very little, save that I could use some food. Then I think I'll take some time playing the clarinet. Can I come up to the bridge?"

"Happy to have you, Star. You can play me your song, the one you wrote in school."

"That'll be nice."

After my shower, after my meal, I sat on the bridge with my feet tucked under me and played my song. I thought of Abigail, who was where she was when she was nowhere, who she was when no one else was there. I thought of Galium and of Honor, two men in my life. I loved both, yet could not stand either in high doses.

I thought of Flax, my benefactor who counted as a crew member, even if most people didn't know it.

We were on our way to Khons, my home, the planet named for the Egyptian god of the chase, where my chase began. Now we were going to chase my father's legacy. He was always fond of riddles.

End

About the author...

Jon Batson is an award-winning author, four-time winner of the Lower Cape Fear Short Story Contest, twice awarded Honorable Mention in the internationally known Writers of The Future Contest for science fiction writers and twice in the Rusty Axe Science Fiction Contest. He makes his home in Raleigh, NC.

For more information about Jon Batson
and to purchase his other books please visit:
http://www.TheRealJonBatson.com
midnightwhistler@gmail.com

Also by Jon Batson

Adventures of a Space Bum
Starlost Child

When **Starwort Bacchus** finds herself running from her landlord, skipping out on the rent, she jumps aboard an automatic repair vessel and hitches a ride to the next port. But the search for her father's legacy, the inheritance her uncle nearly decimated, takes her to planets where friends and enemies are hard to identify and her best ally is a computer. With a pocket full of "Universals" and a ceramic blade strapped to her thigh, she travels the darkness looking for a home. Instead she finds a growing list of places she cannot go to again, including a place she has never been – Earth.

Adventures of a Space Bum
In Search of a Legacy

Starwort continues her search for her father's legacy, carefully avoiding an ever increasing Central Government, an epidemic virus spreading from planet to planet and the ever-present threat of those who seek to steal the legacy. To her and her crew, the promised haven of a home planet seems a dream they will never realize.

Mars Quake

When astronomer Dana Wright thinks she has seen writing on Mars, she wants to take a look through a larger telescope. Senate aide Tom Matthews knows more than he is telling. Tom remembers every one of his past lives and all the people who shared them with him. That is, until he meets Doctor Wright, someone he's never met before. His memory, whether Doctor Wright likes it or not, is the key to the new markings on the Martian surface.

Blue Standoff

When police detective Max Cole buys a DVD from the $2 bin at the discount store, he has no idea that the plot of the movie would parallel his current case, right down to the ex-girlfriend.

The Trasaron Chronicles
Fade to Black

When Earth's population is relocated to a work planet, three unlikely heroes emerge to organize a resistance, dedicated in retaking their home – Earth. This character driven sci-fi saga takes the reader on a page-turning adventure that explores survival, romance and quality of life.

Deadly Research

When author Jack Richmond researches his next novel, he uncovers the biggest conspiracy in history, happening under our noses and in plain sight. Now Jack and his girlfriend are running for their lives. *Deadly Research* is the first novel in the Jack Richmond series.

Research Triangle

Jack Richmond discovers a building on the edge of the Research Triangle where school children were being remotely monitored at a distance for medication reactions. The monitoring room was joyous at the killing of 32 students until the discovery that they were being recorded. Jack Richmond wakes with no memory at all.

Terminal Research

The story continues as Jack Richmond returns home on Halloween to discover his fiancé, Teri, has been abducted. Finding her becomes his first objective, but along the way he has to deal with new assassins, old friends gone bad and members of the organization really running things.

Doll Bodies
A sci-fi anthology

Out-of-this-world tales including other possible futures, space stories, and excerpts from two future full-length projects. If you are craving a little Sci-Fi in your day, here you are. Enjoy!

Nina Knows the Night

Nina Richardson, a mild-mannered law school dropout, is tired of the criminals in her neighborhood. She dresses in black and ventures into the night to become a kick-butt crime-fighter. She discovers her superpowers to be her own inner-strength and purpose.

The Rands Conspiracy

The Rands Conspiracy takes the reader on a Bourne-style chase as Josh and his development team run for their lives after creating an experimental spy-ware program for the powerful, government funded Rands Group.

What they're saying about Jon Batson:

"Jon Batson is not just a writer, but a storyteller. His gift is making you experience what his characters feel and see while he slings irony and witty asides that make others wonder why you're laughing so hard. He looks closer at the ordinary world and determines what extraordinary things a person can do given the right circumstances. The result is a story that won't be put down."

Alice Osborn,
author, editor and teacher of *"Write from the Inside Out."*

"Colorful, engrossing, and highly entertaining! Jon Batson has produced an evocative collection of engaging characters whose lives unfold in amusing, tragic and, often unexpected ways that send the imagination gliding over each one's winding paths, hairpin curves and jarring potholes with the artistic finesse of a truly masterful storyteller."

Karen Michelle Raines, poet/author

"Batson's stories are contemporary yet reminiscent of an earlier time – O'Henry, Raymond Carver and Edgar Allen Poe come to mind. Luckily for us although the aforementioned have gone onto their last edit, Jon will be with us for a long time."

Steven Elliot, Falls River Books

"I could hear you in every sentence. Easy reading, nice payoff, and a few surprises."

Gary Young, Author

"Thanks for writing and sharing your short stories with me. Your characters in these creative adventures come alive with the action and your clean concise writing keep the tales moving at a fun pace! I enjoyed reading them and look forward to more."

J. K. Gildersleeve, Writer and Illustrator

'A good book is one you think about all day and wonder what is happening with the characters, cannot wait to get back to them and hope you haven't missed much while you're away. I found myself emotionally connected all the way through as the story unfolded.'

Susan Henson, Avid Reader

www.ingramcontent.com/pod-product-compliance
Lightning Source LLC
Chambersburg PA
CBHW070546260626
47161CB00002B/522